# Meritage

# Meritage

Collected Works From
Napa Valley Writers
2019

Prose and poetry from members
of the Napa Valley Writers
Branch of the California Writers Club

GVP
Gnarly Vine Press

ISBN: 978-0-9985108-1-1

Print Edition, November 2019
Managing Editor: Geoffrey K. Leigh
Editors: Lenore Hirsch, Marianne Lyon, Kymberlie Ingalls
Editorial Board: Stephen Bakalyar, Judy Baker, Marilyn Campbell, Bonnie Durrance, Jan Flynn, Bo Kearns, Marty Malin, Jim McDonald, Peggy Prescott, and Amber Lea Starfire.
Copy Editing: Rosina Wilson
Cover and Interior Design: Jo-Anne Rosen

Published by: Gnarly Vine Press
Address: P.O. Box 5901
Napa, CA 94581

GVP
Gnarly Vine Press

**Meritage:** Provocative red or white wine blends from "noble" Bordeaux grape varietals. The term combines "merit," reflecting the quality of the grapes, with "heritage," which recognizes the centuries-old tradition of blending, long considered to be the highest form of the winemaker's art. They are considered to be the very best wines of the vintage.

(From The Meritage Alliance, 2019)

# Foreword

This Anthology for 2019 is a collection of written expressions by 33 current Napa Valley writers. The contents are as diverse as the authors themselves, both in age and experience. For some, it is a continuation of their career in writing while others, younger and older, are being published in such a collection for the first time. No matter what the background, the writing includes suspense, humor, connection, surprise, reflection, perspective, insight, love, and wisdom. But none of this would have happened without the leadership of three fine editors: Lenore Hirsch, Marianne Lyon, and Kymberlie Ingalls, as well as those who helped them. Thank you for all your support.

These written articulations are intended for the pleasure and enjoyment of readers, yet they also can bring fresh ideas and feelings delivered through story, verse, and past experiences. Authors write to share, but we also write to create, to express, to transform inner experiences or concepts to external form through the written word. The process itself may involve great struggle, but it can still provide fulfillment to the creator while bringing pleasure to the consumer. The act of creation can produce great satisfaction, bringing to life something that is has been living inside in order to manifest it in physical form. At the same time, it is the desire of the editors and reviewers, who spent many hours in this process, to bring joy and pleasure to readers like you.

— Geoffrey K. Leigh, Managing Editor

It was a pleasure to coordinate the fiction selection and editing. From humor that brought a smile to my face to clever sci-fi and the pathos of historical fiction, these pieces are varied and unique. I worked with a team of five dedicated readers and editors. Bo Kearns and Jan Flynn took great effort to read the submissions with a critical eye and gave meaningful feedback and suggestions, which we shared with the writers. In addition to working on the reading, scoring, and feedback, the following members also worked one-on-one with the writers to refine and polish the submissions selected for publication: Marty Malin, Stephen Bakalyar, Bonnie Durrance, and myself. Creating an anthology is the perfect project for our club, as it gives us all practice in submitting, collaborating, and editing on many different levels. Let's do it again soon!

— Lenore Hirsch, Fiction Editor

What an honor and a joy to have been invited to be the NVW 2019 Anthology's Poetry Editor. The poets featured personify F. Scott Fitzgerald's quote: "We don't write because we want to say something, we write because we have something to say." As you read these magical poems, I hope you will discover for yourself that these writers of verse are all passionately in love with language. Some write of spirit; others chose nature as an inspiration. Still others reclaimed lost passions, and some poems are just recklessly gorgeous,

I want to thank Jim McDonald, Marilyn Campbell and Peggy Prescott for the wonderful afternoons reading, editing and enjoying these buoyant and brilliant verses. I think of Bob Dylan saying: "Poetry is what in a poem makes you laugh, cry, prickle, be silent, makes your toe nails twinkle." I have only one request of the reader, and that is please give each poem more than one reading. I hope that your encounters will open a new door to the universality hidden within. Enjoy, meander, for treasures abound.

— Marianne Lyon, Poetry Editor

What a challenge this was, and opportunity, to volunteer for this project. To be a part of creation is always an honor, and I am always amazed at the unique brilliance to come from each piece of art in all of its forms. What I enjoy most about our true-to-life stories is the feeling that while each life is different, our emotions can be the same.

Thank you to all who entrusted us with your heartfelt words; we read them with care and with hope, and I ask the same of you. Shout outs to Amber Lea Starfire and Judy Baker for their time, patience and insights, and to Lenore and Geoffrey for their guidance. We all had a grape-stomping good time.

— Kymberlie Ingalls, Creative Non-fiction Editor

# Acknowledgments

Like any extensive enterprise, this compilation of prose and poetry was a large group effort. I volunteered to lead it during a board retreat in February of this year, and the Napa Valley Writers Board supported my proposal the next month. Deep gratitude to the board members for trusting me with this project that can create difficult feelings within a group, and it can enhance skills and connections. I truly hope the process we used created the latter.

This publication, however, would never have taken shape without the leadership, dedicated efforts, and support of three fine editors: Lenore Hirsch, Marianne Lyon, and Kymberlie Ingalls. We collaborated on this project with two primary goals in mind. First, we wanted to create a second compilation of short stories, poems, and creative non-fiction essays that would reflect the quality of writing from the members of the Napa Valley Writers. A wonderful publication was produced two years ago, and we wanted to put together a second selection of new pieces to illustrate the continued creativity and quality of work of our members. We thought it also would be a useful way to assist members to improve their writing through suggestions and feedback from the editorial groups.

Lenore Hirsch assembled a group of people to review, provide feedback, and assist in the editing of the fiction submissions. Stephen Bakalyar, Bonnie Durrance, Jan Flynn, Bo Kearns, and Marty Malin were essential in the review and editing process, lending their own experience and insight to support the authors exhibition of their best skills.

Likewise, Marianne Lyon invited Marilyn Campbell, Jim McDonald, and Peggy Prescott to participate in the review, development of suggestions, and editing of the poetry submissions. Again, the time consuming process of reading, rereading, and coming up with editorial suggestions was an important part of the process. This is how we can improve our work as we learn about it through the eyes and experience of others.

For the creative non-fiction submissions, Kymberlie Ingalls included Judy Baker and Amber Lea Starfire to review and make editorial suggestions for those submissions. While there were many good ideas, it also takes time to provide the feedback and review edited manuscripts, sometimes more than once.

I cannot say enough good things about the the leadership and efforts of the three genre reviewers as well as the 10 additional people who volunteered their time to make this idea a reality. From my experience, all of them were committed to a strong publication and assisting authors, where possible, to strengthen their written expression and enhance their writing skills.

I am also deeply grateful to two other people who helped to make this publication more professional. Rosina Wilson spent hours of close inspection with her copy editing to find grammatical and logical inconsistencies, further improving the quality of this work. We very much appreciate her willingness to commit to this project and assist us with her superb skills to help create a higher quality project. I was surprised at how many small and critical issues she found to make our publication more professional.

I also want to thank Jo-Anne Rosen for her wonderful formatting skills and the creation of a cover that makes the publication more appealing. Her formatting was another professional addition to make the layout more consistent and professional. And while a sub-group came up with a few ideas for a cover, it was Jo-Anne who made that a reality. She also is very good at her work, and we are grateful for the contributions of these two professionals.

Finally, I want to thank all those who submitted prose and poetry for consideration and hanging in with the editorial process. I hope this experience helped you with additional ways of creating your work and enhancing your finished pieces. I also hope you as readers enjoy this publication as much as we have done.

— Geoffrey K. Leigh

# Contents

# First Flight:
# Connections

# MOMA Girl

## *Stephen Bakalyar*

Walking the museum's galleries
in my suit, tie, and polished shoes,
I stop at a wall with the projected
image of a dancing teenager.

Lanky limbs and slender torso
devoid of womanly curves
in an undulating, hip-sliding flow
fresh as morning clover.
Moves not sexual but joyful,
the exuberance of youth.
A flickering flame
lost within the music
except for an occasional
self-conscious smile with
dark lips and cloud-white teeth.

Voltage spikes zip down my
optic nerve to the occipital lobe,
where they scatter like crows
from a cornfield to the
alcoves of memory.

Berkeley. The '60s.
I am dancing barefoot in a park,
not with her gracefulness,
but with a fusion of music and soul.
We are the same, this girl and I.
Hey MOMA girl!
You have reminded me
that I once was free.

# Autumn Elegy

*Jennifer Sullivan*

Maureen feels the sand of the driveway grit beneath her sneakers. Slanting rays of morning sun cast shadows below the Doug fir and ponderosa, long dark braids hanging down the back of the mountain.

Meadowlarks pierce the cloudless sky. The last day of her visit—she loves this place, its remote quiet, the Cascades silhouetted to the west. Still, she's tired, worn out, worn out trying to help.

In the upper pasture, her son-in-law Stacey is on the big blue tractor planting winter wheat. The ruffled dirt behind the seeder, soft and dark as chocolate frosting, throws its warm redolence into the air. Maureen breathes it in, the familiar clean smell of the earth. Beyond the cornstalks in the garden, she sees Barb—always Barbara until she left home—surrounded by rows of carrots, cabbages, and greens. In shorts and a halter, she's working with a spading fork. Her broad back and muscled arms are brown; her hair, pulled back in a ponytail, is sun-bleached. Her thick, powerful legs are pushing the fork easily into the dirt, turning out bright orange candles with lacy green flames.

"Good morning, darling."

Barb looks up without stopping. "Hi. Sleep okay?"

"Passed out soon as my head hit the pillow."

"Poor Mom. Well, no work on your last day. You get a vacation."

"Then you'll take the day off, too?" Maureen was elated. She and Barb could drive up to Canada for the afternoon, stay for dinner and a movie. Or visit some of Barb's friends, those artists up the mountain. Or take a picnic and go swimming at Loon Lake. Anything, just to get Barb away from the farm and give them a day together to relax and talk.

"Sorry. No way. Frost's predicted, plus the deer chewed the tops off the carrots last night. If I don't harvest them today, they'll get yucky in the ground. Won't even be able to give 'em away." She pauses in her digging. "If you want, you could trim the ones I've dug. Here. Use these scissors. Leave about a quarter inch of green. Okay?"

"Okay."

Maureen takes the scissors, begins to clip while her daughter moves off to the other end of the row. She wishes Barb would hire a helper. Stacey is always somewhere else, rock picking or disking the fields; making a grain delivery in town. And Robin, beloved granddaughter, is absolutely no help at all, now that she's a teenager. High school. Ballet. Boys. The scissors' snip, snip, snip lulls Maureen as she remembers.

Barb was so pale and thin as a child. Terrible tonsillitis, tonsils the size of walnuts. Always so loving. Threw her arms around anyone who came through the front door. Climbed on the insurance adjustor's lap while he tried to negotiate their claim. Maureen stretches, moves to clip the next row. She remembers coming home from work, Barb running to kiss her, putting little girl arms around her neck and whispering, "I'll be glad when Brett and Katie grow up and leave home. Then I can have you all to myself." Maureen feels those warm kisses where the late-morning sun brushes her cheek. She stops and rolls up her sleeves.

Barb works the spading fork along another row. She glances over at her mother, hoping she's not cutting the tops too short. The carrots have to keep all winter. Barb misses Robin, who's always been her right hand, her loyal helper, twice as fast and just as strong. Two years ago, they did everything together. They were best friends! Then suddenly her darling girl was sixteen, in high school with a life of her own. Without Robin, the work is harder, duller, not fun like it used to be. Barb's begun to hate the garden, chained to it spring, summer, fall, dawn to dark, day after day, cultivating, seeding, weeding, mulching, watering, harvesting. She can't seem to breathe until the first snowfall suffocates the life out of every growing thing. If she'd stayed in school and gotten her teaching credential, she'd be making real money now with a lot less effort. She'd enjoyed practice teaching, being with the first-graders, planning their daily activities. More and more she's been wondering—had she been a fool? Had she made a big mistake? She bites her lips, crushes the thought like a clod of dirt.

The roar of a training jet splits the sky like a visible thunderclap. Maureen looks up, looks over at her daughter. She remembers when Barb, the last of the three, went off to school. Life without teenagers, at last. No rushing to get Katie to her party, to pick up Barbara, to have the car home for Brett. No insisting they change their clothes, put on something clean, something without holes. No watching the clock when they're not home by midnight. Worrying, waiting, imagining. She thought it would be a relief when they finally left home, a big relief. Instead she felt as if she were on a sinking ship and needed a life jacket to keep from drowning.

Barb drops empty baskets along the harvested rows with a series of thumps. "Be careful putting the carrots in the baskets. Don't just drop them in. They bruise."

Maureen begins to fill a basket, thinking how bossy and serious Barb has become. She remembers the fun they used to have when Robin was a baby. Barb was always smiling, ready to do anything, go anywhere with the baby and Grandma. Then she decided to start this truck garden because they needed cash flow. Well, the garden *had* made a little money, but only because Barb put in twelve-hour days.

Maureen helps Barb haul the filled baskets to the gray pickup at the edge of the garden, and they drive to the shop. Behind it, a wide rectangular table sits in a grassy area bounded by choke-cherries and pines.

Climbing out of the truck, Barb says, "You probably don't know that dirty carrots are politically incorrect."

"Can't say it's ever crossed my mind."

"No one will buy them unless they're totally clean. Washing takes forever—you'll see."

Barb again wishes for Robin. Now, she'll have to stop harvesting, take time to show her mother what to do. They'll be working all afternoon. She pauses, feels guilty. She should be taking her mother for a swim or a drive up to Canada…. Well, it can't be helped. Carrots are her big cash crop.

She and Maureen lug the heavy bushels to the table and upend them so that the carrots spill out in piles.

"First you lay them out in rows." Barb arranges a layer of carrots on the wire-mesh tabletop. "Then you wash their faces."

She turns on the hose, sprays a strong jet and, while muddy water runs through the wire, scrubs the carrots, one by one.

"No way can you do this fast. And you can't stay dry. Sorry about that." Barb wipes her hands. "I'll leave you to it while I finish digging."

Maureen grimaces as she massages her back.

"Listen, Mom, if your back's bothering you, don't do any more. I can manage. Go read a book. Seriously."

"Read while you work? No way, José." Maureen smiles.

Barb doesn't smile. "Well I've got to get the carrots washed and into the cooler. If they stay out in this heat, they'll go soft and flabby.

Maureen starts laying out the carrots. "Don't worry. I'll get these little guys ready in no time."

Barb nods, slurps a drink from the hose and drives back to the garden. She wishes she and her mother could get on the same wavelength. She jolts the truck to a stop and picks up the spading fork. She remembers their trip to Mt. Rainier. As they hiked across the glacier, they'd taken turns carrying her pup, Patsy, in their backpacks, worried she'd freeze her paws. What a lark that had been, a week of sleeping among wildflowers, eating the trout they pulled from streams. Why was it so hard to connect nowadays? Because there was no chance for real talk or fun? Because they spent every day mucking around in the garden? First it was two tons of onions, dug and spread out on racks to dry, trailing their leaves like green-haired Rapunzels. After that, the garlic. Thousands of bulbs harvested, prepared for sale, the outer layers of skin rubbed off gently, no nicking, no peeling. Their thumbs and fingers had been chafed raw; their hands had cramped.

Barb looks down the long row, continues digging carrots. She thinks of Robin, still sees her running this morning to catch the school bus, looking so grown-up in a tight pullover—looking like a girl who will soon leave home. She swallows down a lump in her throat. If Robin were here, Barb wouldn't be so depressed, so fed up with her life.

Maureen works on the carrots spread out across the table. She washes and scrubs, washes and scrubs. Mindless, tedious, stoop labor. A stupid way to spend an afternoon. Her back and shoulders ache. She feels so old when she's here. Old and dull, not very fit, not very useful. Not the way she feels at home, running her business, going to parties, cooking dinner with Allan. Never enough time for all the things she wants to do. Here, the hours mire down in garlic and onions and carrots. Still, it's the only way she can be with Barb. She always hopes they'll have some quiet moments together. Sometimes they do. That's kept her coming back.

The afternoon passes. Wet and spattered with mud, Maureen finally finishes. Hundreds of bright-orange carrots without a spot of soil, now dry and put into the cooler. She strips off her soaked jeans and sneakers, flops onto the grass. She feels as if she's been run over by a truck. How does that feel, really? Squashed, flattened, numb? Yes, that's how she feels. Barb floats up behind her closed eyelids. She's in pink ballet shoes, pink tutu, silver leotard, a sparkly silver crown. One of the sugar plum fairies. Too young to be *en pointe,* but she'd wanted the part so badly they'd given in. At the Christmas performance, she'd floated across the stage, her little legs fluttering like bird's wings.

Slanted shafts of fading sunlight fan across the sky. Barb can feel she's been working since five-thirty, and still there's this last load to be washed. She'll have to work fast to finish before dark, get her mother out of the way; she slows things down. Barb drives the truck back to the shop, opens the tailgate, lugs a basket to the washing table. Six hundred pounds since morning—her arms feel like stretched-out rubber bands; her back is howling. She glances at her mother lying on the grass, thin and bony, hair almost white, looking so old. By this time tomorrow she'll be gone. Barb wishes she'd taken a day off. Just one carefree day with her mother to tuck away as a happy souvenir. But frost was predicted....

Maureen opens her eyes. "Ah. The carrot lady. With more carrots." She sits up, gets to her feet, slowly straightens. "What we need is a date with a hot tub."

Barb can see that she's exhausted, walking bent over, kind of gray around the mouth. Not used to this kind of shit.

"No hot tub. How about a hot shower instead? You've done enough for today."

"You're as tired as I am...." Maureen begins to place the carrots in perfect rows.

Barb, rapidly forming a flat orange matrix, needs to hurry. It's getting dark. Her mother is in the way. "Look, Mom. It's too much for you to do any more work. Go on back to the house."

Maureen keeps working. "I'll stay to help finish up."

Barb's face flushes, her mouth tightens. "Dammit, you've worked all afternoon; you've put in your time. I'm in a hurry here and you're in the way." She stares at Maureen and her voice quivers. "You're putting a guilt trip on me."

Maureen looks up, startled. "How am I putting a guilt trip on you? I just want to help you, be with you."

"That's not the way I see it." Barb feels herself falling apart. There's nothing to hang onto. She reaches out, grasps at thoughts that offer themselves willy-nilly. *"You* didn't stop working because *your* mother visited you. Well, *I* have my work too. It may not be in a fancy office with a bunch of people to boss around. But I have customers. They depend on me." She glares at her mother, then begins to sob. "Maybe I'm not the teacher I said I'd be. Maybe I'm a disappointment to you. Maybe you just come up here to feel sorry for me." Tears streaming down her face, Barb sobs, "But this is my life. Maybe you should just get out of it, get out of my life right now and go home."

Maureen, still as a burned-down house, stares at her daughter. She can't move; she can't speak or she'll start crying.

"Go on. Get out of here so I can finish these fucking carrots." Weeping, Barb sprays water across the table's orange mat, starts scrubbing the carrots.

A moment passes. Maureen takes a deep breath, quietly picks up a wet carrot and begins to clean it. Muddy water streams from her fingers through the glistening mesh, down onto the sodden ground. The sun glints on the distant windows of the house, then disappears below the horizon. A silver twilight steals across the fields as the women finally finish.

Barb stands motionless, bent over the table. Maureen shakes the water from her numb fingers, hesitates, then slowly limps to her wet, still tearful child. She tightly wraps her arms around her, kisses her and whispers, "How about a hot shower—and a glass of wine for both of us?"

# When the Big Band Plays Rio Nido

*Lance Burris*

In the summer of nineteen forty-four,
as battles still rage in the Great Pacific War
in lands with place names we never knew,
young men die for the red, white, and blue.
So far away we cannot hear their screams,
as death steals all their youthful dreams.
While in a small river town, where no bombs fall,
other young men answer the siren's call
of the sound of swing from the old dance hall,
as clarinets wail and saxophones moan
to the staggered notes of a slide trombone,
when the big band plays Rio Nido.

It's Saturday night and the sky's full of stars.
The parking lot's full of hump-backed cars.
In the old dance hall, couples circle the room
as the pencil-necked singer commences to croon,
and shiny-eyed girls search for Hollywood love
while a big, mirrored ball slowly circles above,
as clarinets wail and saxophones moan
to the staggered notes of a slide trombone
when the big band plays Rio Nido.

Betty's got painted lips and perm'd red hair,
her sweat-soaked dress perfumes the air.
She wears nylon hose with misaligned seams
as she holds on tight to the man of her dreams.
It's her lover-boy sailor on a weekend's leave.

He wears tight, white pants with stripes on his sleeve.
When the band takes ten, the two duck out.
Soon the sailor's forty-Ford begins to rock
while Betty learns how to tie a sailor's knot
as clarinets wail and saxophones moan
to the staggered notes of a slide trombone
when the big band plays Rio Nido.

# Inspiration

*Lynn Berghorn*

The dramatic sweep of the artist's brush
emits red across the canvas.
Listening as Brahms grandly announces
his First Piano Concerto,
the artist is led into a passionate
merger of mystery and suspense.

Dabbing color from his palette,
he imagines a picture
Brahms is helping him paint.
As the music softens and whispers,
blues and greens appear on the canvas.
The composer is influencing the artist.

While the music dances,
colors are dotted in Seurat pointillism.
Lust, portrayed by red,
combines with a soft mystique,
giving art a feeling:
contemporary romance.

Gathering courage and ideas
from the work of others
is a secret artists know well.
Guided by inspiration,
this artist creates a masterpiece
for God and man.

# If You Were the Friend

*Kymberlie Ingalls*

"Do you ever think about it? Do you ever wonder if he's had an affair?"

"That's random. Is *she* cheating on *you?*"

"Sometimes I almost wish she would."

"Hey, I love you two as a couple. I love us as a foursome. Do you really want that?"

"I don't know."

"I'm glad I went out tonight for drinks after all. I wasn't going to. I'm not into doing social things alone. He's gone 'til Friday, though, and I just didn't want to go home to the empty apartment again."

"I like to sit here and watch people. Kind of my own private thing—nobody here knows me but the bartender. I can use my imagination a little. Haven't done much of that in the last twenty years. The things we sacrifice for the real world and material things."

"I guess that's why I was so surprised to see you here. At first I wondered, being it's a hotel bar and all."

"Those are the best kind for making up stories over cocktails."

"I'll bet! I had a meeting over at the hospital, and on my way back to the train it suddenly seemed appealing to be in a place where everyone is so anonymous and transient."

"Except not so anonymous?"

"Apparently!"

"Have I ever told you how much I love your laugh? It's so free, as though you're never afraid to let go."

"Well, that's an awfully nice thing to say. I'm trying to think of the last time—or *any* time—that we've ever spent time together alone, and I guess we never have."

"No, that's the thing with couples friends. It's permissible for the guys to golf or grab a beer, or for the ladies to shop or do the spa thing—but it all becomes suspect when we begin to mix the genders."

"Suspect? Has she ever had any suspicions about you and me? I can't imagine how she could."

"No, that would take caring on her part."

"Oh, come on now. Is it really so bad as all that?"

"Look, I'm staring at forty-seven through the barrel of a shotgun. We did everything we were supposed to do, and right on schedule. I've provided the cliché that she signed up for—a country club life and a kid who just left for a new life that we did well by. Somewhere in all of that, we forgot how to be alone together. I don't know if it's a matter of rediscovery or moving on. I just know that these cocktails are becoming the highlight of my days, and I don't think that's where I want my life to go."

"I understand. Well, kind of. I'm a couple of years behind you yet. I don't know if we're different, happier even, because we didn't have the kids and the picket fence. All the traveling that we've done, the adventures. I wonder if it isn't too late to grow up and breed before it's too late. People have done it. Sixty is the new forty and all that crap. I think we're unconventionally still in love because of the choices we made, though, and through a turn of luck too. Forming the practice the way we did gave us freedom to do be the hippie doctors doing great things in faraway places."

"Yes, I admit that I'm envious of you two."

"The grass is always greener in the other person's bank account, my friend."

"It isn't just about the lifestyle. I watch the way you look at him."

"She loves you."

"Does she?"

"I would know if she was just using you. I'd know if she was seeing someone."

"But would you tell me? Would you let me live a lie, or tell me the truth if you were the friend, and I were the fool?"

"Of course I'd tell you! Well, I think that I would…."

"You would. You're good people."

"Now I'm sad. I adore you! I'd hate the thought of it."

"But if I ever had an affair, you'd be the first one I'd ask."

"Oh, my."

"There's that laugh again. A guy will say anything to be in your charms, you know."

"Would you tell *me*?"

"Would you want me to?"

"I'm not sure I know the answer to that. Ignorance has its joys. But what is a dishonest happiness worth?"

"It's worth its weight in denial."

"He still tells me that I'm his dream, every single day."

"So, if he were chasing other dreams, should I keep quiet?"

"You're such an antagonist!"

"I actually think that I'm being more honest today than I have been in a very long time."

"Maybe this is why we're not supposed to mix company."

"Because we might speak truths and rat each other out?"

"We say that, but in the end, I think men and women are too loyal to each other. And in our circles, we don't like to break the status quo."

"Unless we have an agenda, and opportunity."

"You're not that kind."

"Aren't I?"

"Oh, stop. You're not! And you can't make me believe otherwise."

"Turn around."

"What? Why?"

"Turn around. Because I have a feeling that you don't know about that woman in the corner that your husband is kissing."

# Simple Pleasures

*Edgar Calvelo*

Two dancers stand opposite each other on the stage, start
Moving in concentric circles, their lines intersect like webs
In space, writing their stories in silent monologues,
I watch their performance. My mind whirls,
Dances geometrically a pantomime with an imaginary friend.

There are things that seem similar:
Maze and labyrinth look indistinguishable.
A parrot can speak on its own. An echo can't.
We can hunt with spear or bow and arrow.
One is easier to learn, the other harder.

Which animal is first to walk the earth?
Which is the fastest, the weakest?

The simple pleasures of watching motions in space,
Spending time with friends and strangers.

I imagine the magnitude of human encounters between
7,401,858,841 that inhabit the earth.

I arrive when the tide has almost emptied the river
A fisherman shows me a photo of his daughter's
Graduation, unaware, a blue heron tiptoes beside him.

A cyclist walks her bike with me, says, her father
Sees butterflies on his bedroom wall every morning,
A narrative that keeps getting longer in length.

I chat with a whistling man. Walking his corgi,
He says, diminishes his disillusionment in life.
He reminds me: "Tomorrow, if you walk, bring water
And an extra step. The whole day may be hot."

The hills are yellowing before me
Even before the summer solstice.
Seedless watermelons are selling for $4.99 each
In the grocery store next to the bank.

Tonight I will read Whitman's Song to Myself
To lull myself to deep sleep on a bed of grass.

# Street Legal

*William Carroll Moore*

Many of the junior and senior students in Modesto High School had cars. But just *any* car in the fifties wasn't enough. Most of us wanted a flashy, smooth, rounded, polished artifact, with a high-performance engine, glittering chrome engine parts, and dual tailpipes. Engine and body modifications and safety features had to produce a racing machine without disqualifying it from DMV registration. It had to remain "street legal." There was lively competition for the most creative paint and customized body work and highest performance engines to contribute to the junior and senior classes' rolling stock. Our cars were also important in dating, and the prettiest, sexiest cars attracted the biggest selection of babes.

But Eddie Rafferty was different from most. In addition to being easygoing and considerate, he was also quietly precise and calculating, and he apparently felt no need to feed some starving ego.

I met Eddie when we both auditioned for and were selected to join our school's a cappella choir. We sat together in the tenor section during rehearsals and, in our solemn robes, stood together during choir performances, sometimes sharing a music folio. Although we got on well together with our music, we had separate circles of friends. As I was in the school's college prep program and he was in the shop and trades program, we shared no other classes, so we seldom saw each other. But I learned to respect Eddie in other ways when I understood his approach to a street-legal car.

Eddie's car was what we called a "sleeper," a deceptive vehicle that looked slow and downright plug-ugly, but was capable of high speeds. The sleeper was cheap to buy and modify, and could even earn cash in drag races.

One Friday night, I was cruising with a friend who was showing off the glittering new candy-apple-red paint and full-moon hubcaps on his modified Chevy, when Eddie pulled up beside us at a stoplight. He was driving an ugly two-door 1940 black Mercury family sedan. It had failing paint and no hubcaps, and it was dirty, but his idling engine had that loping, rolling pattern that sounded like a racing camshaft had been installed. "Is that a three-quarter, or full race cam in there?" I asked.

"Neither one," he smiled. "The engine's so bad I have to advance the idle just to keep the damn thing running." We all laughed and drove on.

"With that junker, he'll never get a date," my friend commented.

A week or so later, I heard that Eddie had won a race out on Paradise Road against a hot rod with all the trimmings— dual carburetors, dual exhaust system, and other modifications. Paradise Road is located southwest of town in an area of dairy farms. The road is straight for a good long distance, and with no houses nearby, it's a favorite strip for car racing. Sometime later I heard Eddie'd won two more races on Paradise, and both had been for money.

On a warm summer evening cruise with my girlfriend, we rolled up to Burge's Drive-In next to Eddie and another boy standing beside their cars, discussing a race. The other boy, Sam, was demanding to see under the hood of Eddie's Mercury before he would agree to a race, so both opened their hoods for inspection. Eddie's engine compartment looked like a black hole compared to the sparkling chrome engine parts of the other car. I could see that Eddie had modified his exhaust system and done something to the carburetor, but Sam wasn't impressed. Eddie wanted to race for pink slips, where the loser surrenders his certificate of ownership to the winner. Sam was cocky enough to like the idea but didn't feel the stakes were a match, given the quality of the two vehicles. And besides, he didn't want Eddie's junker anyway. When the talk moved to cash, Eddie offered $200, but they ended up at half that and asked me to hold their money until the race was over.

I took the money, left my girl with a carful of our friends, and took another boy with me out to Paradise Road. I learned from my passenger that Eddie had generated a small cadre of car lovers who had become gamblers on the races, and money would be changing hands again that night.

We checked in at the starting line, where bets were being made, and the two racers flipped a coin for choice of travel lane. Eddie lost the flip but ended up with the passing lane, which he preferred. We then drove down to where the race was to end and parked off the road. The end team laid a rope across the road for the finish line, and placed flashlights on the pavement beamed on the rope from both sides of the road. The scream of tires in the distance announced that the race had started, and we stood back from the pavement. Eddie's car hit the rope almost two car lengths ahead of the other, and sounded like it was still accelerating as it blew past. Everyone gathered at the finish line. In the beam of lights, all watched as I handed Eddie his money while the others began settling their side bets. We were all working full-time, well paid summer jobs, mostly in fruit and vegetable harvesting and processing, but $100 was still a lot of money for high school boys. And, Eddie was the winner again.

With lights on and all engines idling, we lined up our cars to head back to town. The first car was Eddie's, the second was Sam's, and mine was last. We were engulfed in the heavy odor of engine exhaust and the mellow, throaty sounds from a half-dozen flathead V-8 engines, which make an aquatic "blurble" sound you never forget. Our lineup made a straight bar of light in the country dark as we absorbed the sounds and vibrations, waiting for Eddie's start. Each car left with a rubber-burning slam start, followed by a racking through the gears for quick acceleration to cruising speed. Enough time was left between starts to allow spacing for a high-speed run back to town. I was glad to be last, as my car was slow, and would otherwise have had a racer riding my rear bumper and honking his horn. In town we made a slow parade circling Burge's, where we picked up girlfriends and buddies— cruised through town to Third Street—and headed back to Burge's for hamburgers and cherry Cokes.

Word got around about Eddie's sleeper, so he couldn't get anyone to race him for pink slips. Someone said he was doing some races in Turlock, a town some eighteen or so miles south down Highway 99. One Sunday afternoon I was washing my car in the driveway at home when Eddie drove up in a bright-red '34 Ford coupe I hadn't seen before. When we sat down on the lawn to talk, he said he'd done well in Turlock and hadn't pushed his luck as he had here in Modesto. "Tell me what happened," I said.

"Well, one Friday, I drove to Turlock and challenged someone to a race. I won, getting everyone's attention. The next Friday, I got another race there, which I deliberately lost, and got to know more of the locals. Both those races were for money. The very next night, I went back and got someone confident and aggressive enough to race me for pink slips, and won.

"My God!" I said. "Were you able to collect?"

"You bet. It's the one I'm driving here," he said, tilting his head at the Ford. "I took the precaution of bringing three friends along as witnesses, and to help me collect, if needed."

I noticed when Eddie drove up that the side panels of the hood had been removed to display the engine with all of its brightly chromed racing equipment. He had of course seen it too when he challenged the owner and could judge the car's displayed capabilities. "I pretty well knew what his car could do, and he didn't ask to see my engine before the race. I can add more improvements to this prize coupe and sell it for a good price. Everybody likes the flashy chrome engine parts and the suicide doors."

"What did you do with your sleeper?"

"Oh, I've still got it. I'll be doing some more racing."

I congratulated Eddie on his winnings and asked him to tell me what he'd done to modify his car. It was hard to understand why it was faster than the others, some of which were much lighter in weight. After making me swear not to tell anyone else, he began a description of how he'd built his sleeper. "It had lived its life outside in a dairy barnyard, but the engine had much fewer miles than you would expect, so I started with a good, solid V-8."

"Did you do all the work yourself?" I asked.

"I did most of it so it didn't cost me too much, but I didn't do it all. First I pulled the motor and took the engine block to an auto-machine shop, and had them over-bore the cylinders and install bigger pistons, which gave more power. I installed a full racing camshaft, which makes the valves open and close faster. I pulled off the cylinder heads and had them shaved down at a machine shop, giving me a higher compression ratio for the cylinders, which makes for a bigger explosion when the plugs fire. Adding all that power caused overheating, so I modified the cooling system, adding a bigger radiator, and I wired in an electric fan to keep it cool."

"How much horsepower did you end up with?"

"I don't know, but it's more than anyone else I've raced against."

Eddie's list of modifications included things I hadn't known about before. He was a good mechanic himself, but he'd also had help from his dad, with both tools and experience.

"Had you done all this before racing Sam that night?"

"No. After that, I added dual carburetors, and racing intake and exhaust manifolds. To keep it a sleeper, I didn't put loud mufflers on it, and only one of the dual exhaust pipes went out the back, so the car looked stock. I ended the other pipe under the car so nobody could tell I had a dual system without raising the hood or looking under the car. I didn't use chrome on anything, and whatever was bright, I painted black. Not many racers asked to see my engine before racing, so the sleeper trick mostly worked."

"Are you going to sell one of your cars?" I asked.

"Not yet. I've got more races to run with the sleeper. Everybody knows about me here in Modesto and in Turlock, so this Friday I'm going north to Manteca. I'll end up with some more cash, and with luck, maybe another car with its pink slip. Before school starts this fall, I plan to sell two cars, put the money in the bank and use my sleeper for transportation."

Then, almost as an afterthought, he said, "Forgot to tell you. Talked to the school counselor, and he's helping me get the classes I need to go to college next year. "

"Congratulations," I told him. "You've crossed over from shop and trades to college prep. That's a good decision you've made."

"All my race winnings and car sales are going into my college fund. Next summer I'll have to think of something else for making money."

"Let me know how your races go in Manteca," I told him, as he started the Ford.

"Will do. I'll come by and tell you about it," he said, and slowly blurble, blurble, blurbled his way down the street.

# Pork Ribs With Tomato

*Jim McDonald*

Calabrian recipe handed down
over generations
pork ribs simmer
in bubbling tomato sauce
with garlic and fresh-torn basil.

Lorenzo's family left Italy's boot
poor mountain village
surrounded by turquoise sea.
His father an artist who paints into night
with colors rich as ripe tomato.
His uncle finds dollars like green basil
buying downtown property.

Father modest but creative,
teaches art and paints
dark and bright moods.
The falling-out occurs
when wealthy brother invests
family funds to his advantage.
Children on either side
of fissure become estranged.

Unlike pork ribs with tomato
melding into a signature dish,
two brothers lack a key ingredient
to pull family back together.

# Boots

*Lenore Hirsch*

"Cowboys Forever" by Garth Brooks blasts from the juke-box while the band sets up. Hanna sits down at the bar, orders a draft, and looks around at the crowd. Everyone is wearing jeans. Western shirts and cowboy hats are all around the room. And the boots! Hanna has chosen tennis shoes for comfort, but some of these folks are wearing serious shitkickers.

The country-western bar is in a strip mall near her home in Sacramento, and she is here to line dance. Not that she likes country music—it is too sappy and sentimental; or worse, about Jesus—but she likes to dance. With line dancing, she doesn't have to wait for someone to ask her. At twenty-eight, Hanna isn't expecting to find true love in a bar. She is only interested in dancing for as long as she wants.

Hanna sometimes goes out dancing with her girlfriends. She loves their company, but in a bar they focus on beer and boys. Tonight is about grooving with the music, moving her body, working up a sweat. There is a deep satisfaction in following the sequence of steps; it makes her wish she had taken dance lessons. Dancing makes her feel alive.

She likes coming here alone. Making her own decisions. She was raised by her parents' rules… to be a "good girl." That meant being at home, learning to sew and cook and do laundry while her younger brother was out shooting at squirrels with his pellet gun.

The band finally starts up and the MC takes the mic.

"OK, all you gals and fellas, time to get out here and strut your stuff."

Hanna leaves her half-empty glass and joins in. The instructor takes them through the Boot Scootin' Boogie and the Electric Slide, introducing the steps a few at a time. She has done these dances before and it's easy to follow along. Hanna keeps dancing until she is out of breath and thirsty.

Back at the bar, she finds a guy wearing a cowboy hat seated in her chair.

"Hi," she says, "can I grab my beer?"

"Sorry, want your seat back?" he asks as he hands over her glass.

She wrinkles her nose as she takes a sip of the warm beer.

"Let me get you another one," he says. He signals the bartender. "I'm Bill," he says with a darling smile. Someone moves off the chair next to Bill and Hanna sits down. He turns towards her, one elbow on the bar. He is slim and she guesses pretty tall, maybe six feet. Blonde curls stick out of his hat and his gray-blue eyes look like pools of calm. Around her age, she thinks.

"Hanna," she says. "Have I seen you here before?"

"Maybe. This music sounds like home… I'm from Texas originally."

"You sure don't have an accent," she says.

"I worked on it. I do computer programming, but people treated me like I didn't have a brain. Ah might could talk like a Texas boy if y'all want." And he again gives her that broad smile.

"I'm a teacher," she says. "Eighth-grade English."

"I'd better stick to the correct grammar then, huh?"

Hanna heads back to the dance floor. While she's dancing, she glances in his direction and sees that Bill is watching her. She thinks of Dan for a second, her last breakup, and reminds herself she's not here to meet men. She goes back to the bar to finish her beer. Soon the line dancers begin to depart and the dance floor clears. Bill taps her arm. "Are you ready for a real dance?"

"I'm not sure I know how."

He takes her elbow and leads her out onto the floor. She puts her left hand on his shoulder and places her right hand in his left. His large palm on her waist is so firm that it is easy to follow him around the dance floor. Then he tries some tricky steps that she can't follow. She steps on his foot and nearly trips.

"Sorry," she says, laughing.

"I can take it." He gives her waist a squeeze.

They go back to their seats and Hanna buys the next round of beer.

"Mighty hospitable of you, Ma'am," says Bill. "I don't suppose you would want to go out with me sometime?" There was that grin again.

"I'd like that," she says, in spite of herself.

That's how Hanna gets involved with a country-western-loving computer programmer. He listens to country in his car. He listens to it at home, where she finds herself visiting more and more often. She doesn't have the heart to tell him she can't stand the music. When they are at her place she puts on classical or soft rock, and he seems to enjoy it all. At least he doesn't wear the cowboy hat every day.

Hanna likes having a boyfriend, someone to go with to a movie, or just to crash together in front of the TV after a tough week. She likes talking with Bill, and the times they are quiet. And she likes the sex. Bill takes his time with her, knowing when to make her laugh and when to make her moan. They start spending Friday or Saturday nights together.

Hanna doesn't want to spend more time than that, although Bill is always asking.

"Can you do an early dinner Wednesday night? I'd love to see you."

Hanna frowns into the phone. "Bill, I just can't go out on a school night." She says this even though she does see friends during the week from time to time. On weekends she always leaves his place before breakfast, with lots on her to-do list: laundry, lesson plans, craft projects. She sees her girlfriends every couple of weeks. She likes being in charge and she's trying to keep a balance, but it seems Bill is always asking for more.

A few months later, the winter holidays approach. Hanna's mom is doing her usual nagging about wanting her children home with her, just an hour away from Sacramento, for Thanksgiving. Hanna is feeling guilted into the family thing.

She brings it up one Saturday morning over a quick breakfast at her place. "Bill, do you have plans for Thanksgiving?"

"Hadn't thought about it yet, but I won't be going to Texas until Christmas. Are you going to cook?" Big grin.

"No, but my Mom is. It's just an hour's drive."

"Sounds good."

"Great, but it doesn't mean there's anything serious going on here, right?"

He gives her a quizzical look. Bill thinks everything going on is just fine.

"I mean, I don't want you to give my folks the impression that we're like, you know...."

"Don't worry," he leans over and whispers in her ear. "Your secrets are safe with me."

Thanksgiving is OK—it's the usual crowd of extended family and Bill fits right in. Nobody gives him the third degree. Her mother does take her aside while they're cleaning up for a word of advice, although she thinks it's about her father. "Let him expect his dinner on the table every night at 6:15, and you know what you'll be doing every day?"

Hanna and Bill plan a special dinner at her place a few days before he leaves for Christmas in Texas.

Should they exchange gifts? It would be cheesy to bring it up. She dreads that first-Christmas-together anguish of how much to spend. His gift should be something inexpensive that reflects his interests. She decides on a new CD that has country singers doing a variety of song styles. She likes it and she hopes Bill will too.

After the dinner she has prepared, she presents him with the CD. "Hold on a minute," he says, and goes out to his car, returning with a gift-wrapped box.

"Oh, my," she says. "It's so big."

"Only the best for you."

*Oh, God,* she says to herself.

Bill opens his gift and smiles. He gets up from his seat to hug her shoulders. "I can't wait to play it," he says and goes to her CD player. Her hands tremble as she slowly tears the paper off her box and peeks inside. There she finds, wrapped in soft tissue, a pair of handmade leather cowboy boots, inlaid with pink and red roses climbing a vine. They're gorgeous. She loves them. She hates them.

"I don't know what to say," she says. "You must have spent a fortune." She takes them out and tries them on.

"I just want my girl to look sharp when we go dancing."

Bill stays over and after they have made love and he turns on his side, while she is lying awake thinking about his gift, she hears a whispered, "I love you." She doesn't want it to be true. She thinks about it until she decides she must have been mistaken.

Before Bill leaves town, they talk on the phone about New Year's Eve. The country-western bar is having a party: barbecue, flowing champagne, and a name band. Bill wants to go.

"Couldn't we just go to dinner and a movie?" asks Hanna. New Year's Eve is not her favorite night to go out. And she figures she'll have to wear the new boots.

"Come on, Hanna. It'll be fun. I want to show you a good time."

"OK," she says, then sighs as she puts down the phone.

Bill leaves for Texas, Hanna's winter break begins, and she is thrilled to have time for drinks with two girlfriends. She tells them about the boots. "It's just too much, too soon," she says.

"But I thought you really liked him," says one.

"I do like him, but I'm not ready for a serious relationship, at least not with him."

Her last serious relationship was with Dan. They had been high school friends, sharing the kinds of secrets you do when you're growing up. They went off to different schools for college and saw each other occasionally during vacations, but after graduation they both found jobs back in Sacramento and they reconnected. Dan was Hanna's first real love. Everything was swimmy, and they were talking about moving in together, when Dan went to Chicago for a work conference—and fell madly in love with a woman he met there. He was honest about it when he returned, even apologetic, but in a flash, he was gone to New York and Hanna was left alone.

❧

She wears the boots around the house a few times to break them in. Despite their beauty, they are uncomfortable. Their pointy toes don't match her feet. "Oh, well," she thinks, "I won't have to wear them every day."

Hanna isn't looking forward to the big night. The day before, she stops by a country-western store and buys a red shirt with fringe, thinking it may help her mood. She and Bill will look great on the dance floor. That is as good as it is going to get.

The day of the party, Hanna has a call from a girlfriend. Two of them are getting together to watch a scary movie and order in pizza.

"I wish I were spending the evening with you," Hanna says.

"Come on, girl, you've got your hot cowboy nerd," says her friend, laughing.

"Yeah, I guess. All his idea."

❧

Bill picks her up promptly and gives a low whistle when he sees her outfit.

"Next thing I know, you'll be getting me a cowboy hat!" she quips, realizing right away from the look on his face he doesn't find it funny.

The party is in full swing when they arrive, and they start by filling their plates with ribs and coleslaw and getting a couple of glasses of bubbly. They sit with another couple they know from the bar. The guys talk about their jobs; the girls chat about the band and who's in the crowd. Hanna and Bill dance a couple of times and then the MC announces a short session of line dancing. Hanna perks up. She is eager for the sheer joy of moving in her own space in her own way.

She pushes back her seat to get up. Bill gives her a look.

"You goin' to leave me on mah own, darlin'?" He is smiling, but Hanna feels a wave of disapproval from him.

She grins back, "Yes, I am. I am." And she goes out on the floor.

After a couple of dances, her feet need a rest. Those boots are pinching.

"You and your line dancing," says Bill.

"What about it?" she asks.

"I just don't get it, that's all." It's just before midnight and the band starts a slow song. Bill takes Hanna to the dance floor. He embraces her gently and she holds on. 4... 3... 2... 1.... They kiss to welcome the new year, but Hanna is ready to call it a night.

They are quiet on the way home. They've decided in advance to stay at Bill's house. Hanna is sitting on the bed pulling off the boots with some effort when Bill sits down next to her.

"What's with you tonight?" he asks.

"What do you mean?"

"Didn't you like the party?"

"If you haven't figured it out by now, I like to dance, but I really don't like country western music or your stupid hat and you shouldn't have given me these expensive boots and they're killing my feet." Hanna bursts into tears.

"Where's this coming from?" he asks. "I thought you liked me." She shakes her head, unable to speak. He sits down beside her.

"I do like you, Bill. It's just more than I can handle right now."

He puts his arm around her, but she wriggles free and turns away. "I thought we were doing fine," he says.

"Maybe you should ask what I think more often."

"All right," he says. "I'm going to have a nightcap. Are you interested?" She musters as much calm as she can and mutters, "No, thanks." Bill leaves the room.

Hanna throws off her shirt and jeans and crawls into Bill's bed. She is asleep before he returns.

Hanna wakes early. She looks at Bill's peaceful face on the pillow. The stubble of his beard, his long lashes, the blond curls in disarray. She tiptoes around the room, putting her clothes on—shirt, jeans, boots. She leaves a note for him on the kitchen counter. Stepping out into the frigid air, she inhales deeply, stretches her arms. She opens her car and throws in her purse, then pauses. She walks back to the front door, removes the boots and leaves them on the porch, then walks in her stocking feet back to her car.

# Nasturtiums

*Marianne Lyon*

Come with me
    into my garden of nasturtiums.
        Their faces a fiery palate of color,
          round bouncing leaves

like china-tea plates
    that dutifully held cookies
        for my baby dolls
          each summer afternoon.

Come with me
    spend some time
        with nasturtiums abundant.
          They are story keepers

waking and finding
    sun scrambling on dewy grass
        listening to afternoon rain
          falling like a soothing murmur.

Let them fasten your gaze.
    Yoke a sacred communion.
        Give them your eyes
          rayed with smile lines.

See how they dance on whimsical breeze
    full of seed, full of possibilities.
        Listen, a good report comes from
          satisfied hummingbird.

Come with me
    into my garden of gently shaking nasturtiums.
      Get lost in their rustle-talk
          watch sun transform them into light

# Marbry

## *Stephanie Hawks*

Her name was Marbry, and she was my mother. She lived up to her unusual name by being bigger than life—which came out in spades whenever she sat down to play the piano. I've never seen or heard anyone ever play the way she did. We had a Chickering square grand; an antique upright made by Collard and Collard of London; a small, sixty-four note Marco Polo that we could haul down to the beach and sing around; another old upright we kept outside; and the one Mom played the most because of its location in the kitchen. It was a Baldwin console painted white. We had so many because Mom might want to sit down at any given time and play a song, which she did—frequently.

She played totally by ear in a honky-tonk barroom style, with her size 10½ double-A right foot keeping the beat on the sustain pedal. Her left hand would play a modified stride bass. Mom would play the top note of the octave with her thumb; her pinky would play the lower note; her wrist would go down as she did this—and then she'd move her hand up an octave to play a chord. Her right hand would play the melody, with parts of the chord mixed in. She had long, slender fingers that could reach an interval of a tenth—with fingernails painted red and long enough that we could hear them click when they came in contact with the tops of the keys.

Her body was in constant motion; her playing was loud and matched in volume by her singing—full of energy. She always had her cigarette and a glass of vodka perched on top of the piano. There was nothing subtle or quiet about the way my mother played. Her hands would glide from one spot to the next as if she were gathering up the notes and depositing them to the middle of the keyboard.

These sing-a-longs we'd have would often start by someone sitting at the kitchen counter, drinking coffee with Mom, and asking her if she knew some song. Mom would immediately go to the piano and start playing it. Sometimes, there would be some hunting and pecking to find the correct melody until she had figured out how it went. This would lead into another tune, and off we'd go. It could end as soon as it had started. If Mom had been in the middle of a project when she sat down, she might jump up and go finish what she had been doing, and that would be that.

Other times, during a party, we might be singing until midnight or later. Since we didn't have pages for us to read the words or notes while we sang, we learned all of the songs by ear as well. If someone didn't know the words, Mom would turn around and look back as she fed us the words to the next line—while simultaneously playing the part we were singing—and she never missed a beat. It was hard to imagine the vast repertoire she carried in her head.

She played everything in the key of C, and the rare times she had to play a sharp or flat, I made fun of her by saying "Look out, Mom, you're playing one of the black keys." She had a gift for engaging and connecting to people through her music, and the freedom that came with being unencumbered gave way to a joy and total abandonment she shared with everyone.

My mom died in 2000, and with her went all of the shared musical experiences, because no one was there to replace her. I keep these experiences and memories alive by visualizing her playing the piano while I silently sing along in my head.

Her name was Marbry, she was my mom, and she played the piano.

# Simple Love Poem for Candice

*John Petraglia*

**1.**

Missing you
At three a.m.
My arm reaches for
Rests on your pillow.
I stretch my leg
Over cool sheets
To your side of the bed
Seeking your warmth
In my life
Day and night.

**2.**

Of the many things
I cherish about you
How you say *yes* is a favorite.
A mindful affirmation
Soft, stressed, sweet, slowly sibilant.
Somehow you make it two syllables
Or a long drawn one
Rising then falling to a disappearing end.
Worth savoring, extraordinary *yes*.
And yes too, your bangs framing your eyes.

**3.**

Saturday morning serendip.
The whoosh sound effect
of your incoming text
Nudges me awake

As I half listen to the radio
And shift in the cool morning air.
Good morning lover
From three times zones away.

# The Holster

*Stephen Bakalyar*

As Fred Ashton browsed the magazine shelves, he became aware that the woman standing next to him had a holstered pistol on her hip. He turned and stared at it. Gun in a bookstore. It took a moment for the cultural dissonance to dissipate. He had arrived in Austin yesterday. It was the first time he had encountered the Texas open-carry law.

She looked up and stared hard at him.

"Oh, I'm sorry," he stammered. "I'm from San Francisco. Not used to guns. I mean, seeing guns... in a book store."

Her eyes softened. "Of course. I was in City Lights last year. No guns." She smiled.

"Yes. City Lights. A wonderful store, but this place beats it, don't you think?" She turned back to the magazines without answering. "Say, would you like to...."

"I don't think so," she shot back.

"Sure." He started to walk away, but stopped. He was at BookPeople to research an article he was writing on independent bookstores. But it occurred to him that a piece on gun laws might interest his editor even more. And he had noticed she wore no ring. He turned back. "Sorry to bother you again. I was going to ask if you would join me for coffee. I'm writing an article on gun laws and thought you could give me an interesting perspective." She said nothing. He waited. "It would really help me out."

Silence. Finally, without looking at him, she said, "Meet me in the cafe in ten minutes."

"Ten minutes. Great." He went upstairs, selected a table, and scribbled "Austin gun lady" in his notebook. He stood as she appeared at the top of the stairs. The black pistol and holster were conspicuous against tight-fitting red jeans on long legs. She struck him at first as a mischievous young woman—bright blouse, unbuttoned at the neck, and black hair with a gamine cut. But as she approached, he judged her to be about forty. He wondered what the demographics were of women who openly wore sidearms.

"Thanks for coming. I'm Fred Ashton." He handed her his card, hoping the San Francisco Chronicle logo would reassure her that he was a professional journalist.

"Jean Hall." She shook his hand, put her large gold purse on a chair, and sat down.

Ashton picked up his pen. "I'll take notes if you don't mind." She nodded.

"I'm interested in why you wear a gun."

"Well, I'd rather not say. It's very personal. But I'll be happy to tell you about my pistol."

Ashton learned about her Smith and Wesson M&P40: its strengths, limitations, and popularity compared to other models. He liked her clear and relaxed manner of speaking and the way she kept her hazel eyes fixed on his, even while sipping her coffee. He was eager to learn more about her. "Do you come here often?"

Hall hesitated, and then continued. "It's my favorite hangout. I love books and write a little myself. That's why I was at City Lights. When I started writing I got interested in Beat poetry, especially Ferlinghetti. He started City Lights. Well, you know that." For nearly an hour they talked about writing and the novels they were working on.

Finally she said, "I have to go. I've enjoyed talking with you, Fred." She shook his hand firmly. "I hope I was helpful. Good luck with your article."

He watched as the holster, its pistol, and the tall, appealing body on which they hung sank from view down the stairs. The thought of not seeing her again annoyed him. The next day, after interviewing the store manager, he left the store and saw a woman in red jeans getting into a car. He ran. The engine started as he tapped on the passenger window.

Hall smiled and stabbed a finger at her wrist watch, flipped on the turn signal, and put the car in drive.

He tapped harder. She stared ahead for a moment, then moved the shift back to park, and cracked the window. He bent down. "Hi, I thought it might be you. I was hoping we could talk again. As I read over my notes, I saw I had more questions."

"More questions," she said, flatly. "Well I'm really very busy today and late for an appointment."

"Sure, sure. So how about next time you're here?"

She looked at her lap, then turned to him. "I might be back tomorrow." She reached into her purse and poked a card through the window. "Call me in the morning if you want."

"I will. I'll definitely call you." He stepped back, and she pulled out into the traffic. He looked at the card. The image of a police badge jolted him. Back in his hotel room, a search on Google and the Austin police website increased his curiosity.

At police headquarters, Hall changed from heels to flats, put a jacket over her blouse, and went to her desk. She checked out Ashton on the computer. He had lived in San Francisco all his life, written for the Chronicle for several years, published three books, was divorced, and lived with two rescue dogs. Nothing she learned was off-putting, and after thinking about yesterday's conversation she realized that she liked this man.

The next morning Ashton waited until 8:10 to call her. "Hi, it's Fred. San Francisco."

"Oh, hi, Fred. I'll probably be at the bookstore around ten o'clock today."

"Great. I really appreciate this. Hope you come."

He found her in the biography aisle. She led them to a table in the cafe's back corner. In their previous conversation, she had learned that he had never owned a gun. Yet he seemed to have a fascination with them. She looked around. There were only two other customers, a young couple holding hands across the table.

"It occurred to me you might like to examine my pistol." She eased it out of the holster, set it on the table, and pushed it toward him. "Don't worry. It's not loaded."

His stomach tightened. It might as well have been a cobra. "Isn't it against regulations?"

"To give it to you? Yes. To have it unloaded? Under normal circumstances, yes."

He lifted it up and down to gauge its heft. It fit comfortably in his hand and seemed a natural extension of his arm. As he turned the black object to examine every part, he realized that it was capable of giving him a sense of security, perhaps even a feeling of power. There was an unpleasant friction between this epiphany and his anti-gun attitude. It reminded him of the conflict between his contempt for the country's militarization and the thrill of watching the Blue Angels roar low over San Francisco Bay.

Ashton handed back the pistol. To keep his journalistic cover, he asked her observations about the gun culture in Texas. Then he turned the conversation to her personal history and finally said, "Why didn't you tell me you were a cop when we first met?"

"In these clothes you would have had a lot of questions. Things I didn't want to discuss, and that would not have helped your article."

"I get that. But, I do wonder what kind of police work you do, and... well, about how you dress. I mean, you look fantastic."

She thought for a moment, then said, "Fred, I am seeing you again, not because I wanted to help with your article, although I wish you well with it, but because I think you might be able to help me. First, I'll tell you what's going on. There was a rape in this neighborhood. In the early morning. She was walking by the park and was wearing a sidearm that was conspicuous. The chief has a theory that the guy gets off on assaulting women who wear guns. I think it's far-fetched and told him so. But he asked me to be a decoy." She fingered the frills on her sheer blouse.

"He knows my martial-arts skills. I really do know how to kick ass. He gave me the opportunity to refuse, but I like this kind of challenge. So here I am in the morning, walking the streets, in this ridiculous outfit."

Ashton took a moment to grasp what she said. "It sounds risky."

"I can handle myself. If the guy grabs me, he'll be visiting the ER on his way to getting booked." She said it without bravado. "I have a squad car not far away backing me up. It's unlikely anything will happen."

"God, Jean, I hope not. So, tell me what I can help you with."

"You're going to wonder why I would tell this to a stranger. But I...."

Ashton leaned forward. "Hey, Jean, we're buddies. I've even played with your pistol." He flashed a smile. "And there are no secrets between writers." He was pleased at this made-up aphorism and excited at the prospect of increased intimacy.

"OK, here's the deal. In two months I will have worked for the department twenty-three years and be able to retire at three-quarters pay. It will help me do what I have wanted for a long time." She searched his eyes for something that might give her either pause or confidence. It was a futile inquiry. She placed both hands on the table. "I'm going to change my gender."

Ashton squinted his eyes. "What?"

Hall waited. Let it sink in. "I'm going to start living as a man."

Ashton's lips slightly parted.

"I know. Not what you expected," she said.

"Jeez no. I mean... why?" He looked down. "Sorry, none of my business."

Hall said, "I have always felt more like a man than a woman. Now I'll openly live as one. I'm not going to have surgery. That's difficult, especially for someone my age. But I am going to change my appearance. Hormone therapy will help."

She allowed more silence, then said, "I'm going to move to San Francisco. Austin is…."

"You're moving to San Francisco?"

"Yes. I like Austin. It's liberal, for Texas, but I think the Bay Area would be a good place to start over, so to speak. I've been in touch with transgender organizations in San Francisco. There is a lot of support there. But it would be helpful from the get-go to have a male acquaintance there, especially a fellow writer. You obviously know your way around the city. I realize it takes a lot of, well, *cojones*"—she smiled—"but I am asking if you would consider staying in touch before and after my move."

Ashton sat back in his chair. "Oh man. I was… I was… looking for a girlfriend." He tried to keep a cheerful face and hide his disappointment. He raised his arms. "But, what the heck. I'll settle for a just plain friend. Jean, I'll be glad to help. How about a drink tonight, and we can talk about it?"

"That sounds great, but let's make it dinner. Uchi is a good Japanese restaurant. Does six o'clock work for you?"

"Works fine."

Hall pushed her chair back. "I've got to go. See you tonight."

Ashton watched her descend the stairs. He had a faint feeling akin to arousal, but dulled. He wondered if she was really as attractive as his first impression. One thing he knew. She could no longer be an object of his desire.

Three weeks later, while walking the dogs, he received a text. "Retired my red jeans. I got a sprained ankle and black eye, but the guy is lucky to be alive. I'm emailing a draft of chapter two. Look forward to your comments. Let me know when your piece in the Chronicle comes out. See you after my house gets sold. Jean. (It's a male name on the European continent. Maybe I will keep it!)"

# Lost Fantasy

*Antonia Allegra*

It was in the wheat fields near Chartres
That the beauty of the land sang to me.

I felt the exhilaration of a farmer
looking at the fruits of his struggles,
tall and greeny-yellow,
coloring the earth for miles.

I knew the simplicity of a grain of wheat,
its reedy stem and peacock-featherhead
flapping against hundreds of mirror-images
with the sound of Japanese fans opening and closing.

I understood the desire to be one with the earth, with the wheat,
   with you.

Had the rushing wind not been so cool,
Had the children not been bobbing nearby
in their new-found hide-and-seek fairyland,
I would have come to you and explored
the beauty of our bodies locked with the land.

Now the wheat still grows near Chartres cathedral
And my fantasy remains, never to be fulfilled.

# The Master Trapper

*William Carroll Moore*

My friend Junior and I were getting better with our slingshots. After practicing with cans on a fence and an occasional blue-bellied lizard kill, we couldn't get close enough to birds or rabbits to get a good shot. "We're tolerable good at shootin', but we can't hit anythin' big enough to eat," Junior said.

We wanted to get something we could bring to the table for food. We might have put our efforts into fishing, but there was no river or creek nearby with decent-size fish. In our local streams, we could only find crawdads, which were tasty little creatures, but we never caught enough for anything like a meal. Our fathers wouldn't allow us to have guns for hunting, so our thoughts—and curiosity—turned to trapping, something neither of us knew much about.

We had both tried what we called "box traps," where you prop up a basket or other container with a stick, tied to a long string, leading to the hidden trapper. After spreading bait, usually bread crumbs, in a trail leading to more bait under the basket, the trapper waits for the birds, squirrel or whatever creatures to be lured in. A yank of the string trips the trigger and the basket falls over the prey.

Neither of us had caught anything with such contraptions. I had once thought I would freeze to death lying in the snow, with a trigger string in my mittened hand waiting for snowbirds to take the bait—only to lose them when I lifted the trap. Junior and I agreed we needed a better system.

After some discussion, Junior allowed as how he had a kinsman, a Mr. Scarlett, who knew "everythin' about trappin'." He had trapped for pelts in his earlier years, and Junior claimed that he was, in fact, a Master Trapper. Junior soon arranged for us to meet with him for a consultation after school one day, out front of Junior's family barn.

When we arrived, Mr. Scarlett was standing near a wooden bench next to the barn, looking absent-mindedly off into the horizon, but in such a strange way that I had the feeling he was seeing well beyond it. He was a square, heavy-set fellow with gray hair and beard, dressed in farmer's blue-denim bib overalls and a blue shirt. The sun-darkened skin of his face looked stiff as whit leather, and it emphasized the brightness of his pale-blue eyes. Junior, usually a good talker, introduced us—but then fell silent, leaving the consultation to me.

Scarlett sat himself down heavily onto the bench, leaving us standing in front of him. He slowly shifted his weight onto one buttock, released a long, high-pitched fart that ended in a question mark and, pleased with himself, smiled and said, "Now then. You boys want to learn how to trap small animals."

Junior didn't respond. I said: "Yes sir. Our daddies won't give us guns yet—we're too young. We want to trap some rabbit and squirrel, and maybe a big bird or two."

"Have you heard you can catch grouse by sprinklin' salt on their tails?" Scarlett asked with a smile.

"Yes sir, I've done heard that one," I said, returning his smile.

I sensed that Scarlett was skeptical of our ability to follow through on anything he might tell us.

"Well," he said, "trappin' is a complicated thing, you see. You have to know a lot about the animal your're workin' with before you can even start. If it's a bait-set trap, you have to know what it eats, and if the bait has to be live or dead. If it's a trail-set trap, you have to know where he travels every day, or days, and what time he walks the trail."

Scarlett described homemade traps as being of two kinds—deadfalls and snares—and said that either can be made by a trapper using only a good pocket knife, a hand ax, and some stout cord.

"I like the deadfall best," he said. "For a deadfall, you build a bait pen by drivin' saplin' stakes well into the ground in a square or circle pattern, and cover it with saplin' logs weighted down with rocks. To reach the bait, the animal has to enter the pen at a small openin' where you set the trigger. When it's triggered, a suspended weight, a log or rock, falls on the animal, killin' it instantly."

Ending his last sentence, he brought his right hand down on his left with a loud clap. He ticked off the advantages of the deadfall: "It's the most humane way to kill the animal; they die instantly with no warnin' to others; doesn't damage the pelt; no cost; no weight to carry along the trapper's trail—and they can be reused. The deadfall is so quick," he continued, "I've killed skunk without their ever leavin' a scent."

This was getting complicated. Pelts are fine, but I wondered if we could eat an animal that had been squashed by a rock. There must surely be a simple trap or snare for a squirrel or rabbit. The snares Scarlett described sounded even harder to do. His favorite example was a spring-pole snare; a noose made of wire or stout cord.

"You scout out the animal's trail, find and strip a saplin' beside its path, and bend it down and connect it to the snare with a baited trigger device. When triggered, the saplin' snaps back up, holdin' the noosed animal—which hangs there till the trapper comes back to take it."

I couldn't imagine snaring a squirrel and having him hang there crying for a day or so before I skinned him to eat. It was pretty clear we wouldn't be able to do any of the trapping Scarlett described, especially his trigger mechanisms. From his descriptions, the triggers were hand-carved devices that might have required both skill and years of practice to make. Junior seemed to be on the same thought path when he finally found his voice.

"Did you ever use these traps and snares to catch squirrels or rabbits?" Junior asked.

"No," Scarlett said. "I shoot squirrels and rabbits. I used the traps to get marten, mink, ermine, fox, coon, and a couple of beavers one time."

I had heard of but never seen most of the animals he described. Except for coon and fox, I was sure they didn't live here anymore.

"I used to shoot turkey too," he said, "but we don't have them here no more."

I thought the steel traps, like the ones I'd seen hanging in my uncle's barn, might be the best thing for squirrel and rabbit, so asked Scarlett about them. As I asked the question, a darkness came across his face. After hesitating a bit, he said:

"You boys don't want to do that. Steel traps are bad. You might catch your own dog, or somebody else's dog, or your brother or cousin." Scarlett told us how he had seen where animals caught in steel traps had gnawed a leg off below the trap jaws to escape. He mentioned, too, that some trappers set steel traps underwater to catch beaver, which killed the beaver by drowning. "Just imagine a water animal like a beaver dyin' that way," he said.

I thought it awful, too, animals gnawing their leg off to get free, and beavers being drowned. The Master Trapper continued his disdain for steel traps by describing how trap makers had devised a webbed jaw trap, which would prevent the animal from gnawing its leg off to get free.

"I don't trap any longer," Scarlett said, trying to bring some brightness back to the conversation.

"I just hunt sometimes," he added.

"Why did you stop trappin'?" Junior asked.

"Two reasons, I guess. The animals have been drove out by clearin' for farmland, and the ones left over have been trapped-out with steel traps." This seemed to be the end of his answer, but Junior persisted. "What was the other reason, sir?"

"Hard to explain," he said. "When you get to know the animals like I did, they get to be close and  personal. Some of them that took a while to catch got to know me too. We were enemies, workin' for our own survival, and we both knew it."

Struggling to his feet, he said: "I have to leave you boys now. I've got pigs to feed. I'd advise you both to wait a while, till you can shoot a rifle or shotgun—and in the meanwhile, get your daddies to take you huntin' with them. You boys won't be needin' any traps."

After saying his goodbye, he left us, his eyes resuming the far-off look of one who has always lived wild and apart. Our Master Trapper turned and headed for his horizon.

# You Belong Here

*Carole Malone Nelson*

Clouds drape a mask over moon's full face
low in the western sky, end of a long night's journey.
Glistening path on the sea beckons, come aboard,
it's better here, you belong here.

If I follow its lure, will I find you?
Are you there, but I just can't see?
Is the curve of the earth on the far horizon
as close to heaven we living are allowed?

A restless sleep with dreams
part fantasy, part nightmare.
You're here, you're gone, you're gone forever.
Don't go, come back I scream out loud.

Gentle roar of the ocean muffles my cry.
It doesn't know how much I hurt,
doesn't care.
But, it doesn't know how much it helps.

Morning light, even birds still sleep,
but not for long.
That peaceful moment before I remember,
before sorrow courses through every cell.

The brilliance of the sky, sun, and sea,
hurt my blurry eyes.
I close them tightly.
Now, I can't see the beauty, but I feel it.

A deep gasp of tropical air inflates my starving lungs,
softens the sharp edges that slice,
whittling away at knot deep in my belly.
I've forgotten to breathe.

Kaua'i nei with the promise of aloha,
gentle, kind, healing, always healing.
Relax, breathe, trust, let go.
It is better here. I do belong here.

But you belong here with me.

# Evolution of an Innocent

*Rose Winters*

---

*Eleven p.m.* Deidre slipped out of bed. She picked up her stockings from the floor and washed them in the bathroom sink. They weren't really dirty—she had no sweat glands or pores—but she liked the ritual. It made her feel human. She rinsed them and hung them on her shower bar. Twenty minutes before, she'd had company in that shower. A beautiful man, as perfect as if he'd been manufactured at the android plant like herself. His hair black and silky to the touch, his skin smooth. He had a smoldering smile. His pheromones were real enough. There was something about the smell of human males that gave her pleasure.

She lifted her arm and took a pointless sniff. Androids were still scentless, though there had been debates lately on whether or not to add a pleasant non-allergenic odor to them.

Deidre slid on a silk robe and walked back to bed, smiling at the curious sight. John had a pillow over his face. Humans had the most peculiar sleeping habits.

She pulled the pillow away. "John?"

He didn't stir.

She touched his cold face, concerned. "John?" She concentrated on sound. She heard the *whooshing* of a train on the metro rails twenty floors below. That was all. No heartbeat, no breathing, except her own.

She placed her fingers against his neck to feel for a pulse. "John?" she repeated, even though her logic program suggested it was pointless. He was obviously dead—the black-haired man named John.

She sat beside him on the bed, greatly concerned. A dead man in an android's apartment would have repercussions. *And*

54

*why was there a pillow on his face? Had he died of asphyxiation?* There would be inquiries, and she would surely be taken apart and examined. She did not like that thought at all.

"Logic chip: Set to 100%." Deidre felt her focus sharpen.

She went over the facts.

*John came to my door this evening at 9:13 p.m. He appeared to be in peak physical condition. He visited my bedroom and I provided him with romantic services. He showed no signs of distress. He seemed content and healthy all evening.*

Deidre said aloud, "Play memory record: March 12, 2050, 10:15 p.m."

Deidre's eyes projected the evening's prior events onto the wall. She leaned forward, listening and watching.

John smiled, his head nestled into a pillow. "You are quite beautiful, Deidre."

Deidre heard her earlier self respond: "Thank you. So are you, John." She laid her head on his chest.

Deidre listened carefully to the recording. John's heart rate was a steady 63 beats per minute. No telltale sign of a heart murmur, irregular breathing, or any other anomaly. He didn't appear to be in any pain.

"Memory record: Advance 25 minutes."

The projection showed a 10:40 p.m. time stamp, and John in the shower, washing his hair and laughing with her.

"Memory record: Advance 15 minutes."

10:55 p.m. John lay next to her in bed, smiling at her. He said, "I enjoy your company Deidre. I'd like for us to be friends."

"I'd like that, too." She turned out the lights and the screen went dark. John chatted about his favorite music, called jazz.

Time stamp: 11:01 p.m. And they were still chatting in bed. *But I was washing stockings at 11:01 p.m.*

Deidre's eyes widened. Androids were programmed to show an expression of surprise when they came upon a puzzling equation. But Deidre felt genuinely alarmed. She realized there was an anomaly in her memory records. "Current time and date stamp on my mark. Mark."

"11:43 p.m. and six seconds, March 13, 2050.

*March 13th? I'm missing a day.* "Memory record: Play last recording before missing data."

In the dark she could hear them both breathing as if asleep. Time stamp: 12:00 a.m. The screen blipped off.

Deidre became acutely aware that she was in trouble. A missing day of memories meant it was very likely that she herself had caused John's demise. Every subroutine in her neuro-circuitry told her to call the authorities and turn herself in. She imagined herself being pulled apart. They would start with her head, and they would undoubtedly keep her awake so they could ask her questions. They would shut down her motor functions so that she would lie there with no control, no ability to run, push them away, fight….

She noticed her heart racing. Androids *did* have a cardiovascular system, which was programmed for rapid heartbeat given certain stimuli. Fear of death was not one of them. An android with a fear of death could potentially be dangerous to humans.

"I am malfunctioning."

*I am frightened.*

She felt a hot drop of liquid on her cheek. At first, she thought she had been injured and was leaking fluid. She stepped over to the mirror and saw tears. She was not programmed for tears. She had no tear ducts. She leaned close to the mirror and pulled down her lower eyelids. And she saw them. A little hole in each inside corner of her lower lids, that hadn't been there before. Tear ducts.

Her pulmonary system abruptly processed excess air into oxygen.

*I am hyperventilating. How is this possible? What is happening to me?*

She studied her reflection, her contorted expression of panic.

"Self-diagnostic on my mark. Mark."

Her eyes projected her vital signs as a hologram.

Aside from the elevated heart rate and respiratory imbalance, she was running at peak efficiency. "Close diagnostic."

She returned to John and examined his body. There was nothing in his mouth, no wounds on his body, nothing broken. No froth or spittle to indicate poison. Her only conclusion was that she had smothered him with a pillow.

And, in a strange act of self-indulgence that was certainly not part of her program, she pulled his lower lids down and examined his tear ducts. They looked just like hers.

*Am I human then?*

In that fleeting moment, she almost believed she was. But humans didn't have holographic diagnostic capabilities, nor projectors built into their eyes. What had happened in that lost day? Had she killed someone? Had she… evolved? The two questions juxtaposed made her realize something horrible. Unspeakable.

*Unspeakable? I am an android. But I am thinking like a human.*

The unspeakable thought was that, in killing, she could not have evolved, but devolved into something that was not meant to be.

I am a monster.

Something had happened to her, physically. Something that could not be explained through logic. A gift? No. A curse. She was a bad android. Worse, she was a bad… person. She thought again about turning herself in, about lying on a table, unable to move as they poked and prodded. What if they never turned her off, but left her on that table in pieces? Or what if they turned her off and she stayed sentient? Able to think, unable to communicate?

The torturous thought caused a madness in her that she simply couldn't bear. She placed the pillow back over John's face and whispered, "Deidre program: Off."

Nothing happened.

"Diagnostics: Erase Deidre program."

Nothing happened.

Her face grew hot with tears. She felt her face tighten with sorrow. Her voice quavered. "Terminate Deidre android."

Still no change.

She walked out to her balcony and closed the door behind her. She looked over the ledge. The railway was directly beneath her, twenty floors down. If she jumped and aimed her cranium for the tracks, there would be no chance of her program surviving that. The trains came every two minutes. Her timing had to be just right. She calculated gravity and distance. "Time stamp, on my mark: Mark."

"11:58 and 3 seconds."

She stepped to the ledge.

Billy Johansen unlocked Deidre's door and burst into the apartment. "We are *so* late—they wake up at midnight. Hurry!" He trotted into the bedroom.

Sam followed in his white lab coat, beaming. "If the John series passed the test, we're rich. Do you think he fooled Deidre? Do you think she believed he was human?"

"Only one way to find out." Billy reached into John's mouth and pulled out a tiny silver chip from his back molar. "I got the data."

Sam sniffed the air. "I wonder if Deidre noticed the new scent on the John unit." He pointed, "Why was that pillow on his face?"

Billy chuckled. "Because that's how I sleep, and I programmed him."

"You're a strange guy." Sam searched the apartment. "I'm curious if Deidre noticed her upgrades. I'm especially proud of the tear ducts. And the emotion enhancement. Uh… Billy? Deidre's gone."

Billy frowned. "She's not in the apartment?"

Sam shook his head, worried. "No."

"You set her waking timer for midnight, right?"

Sammy nodded. "Yeah. Well, for 24 hours." His eyes widened. "Daylight savings time. I forgot."

"So she's already awake. Since eleven p.m."

"But where did she go?" asked Sam, raising his voice over the sound of the train.

# Breakfast at Ajijic

*Lance Burris*

My father loved to drive. He wasn't a car nut; he just loved to drive and did so as fast as circumstances would allow. By fast I mean in excess of one hundred miles per hour. When I was a child, he would put me on his lap and place my small hands on the steering wheel. Then, at a high rate of speed, he would drop the right front tire off the pavement in order to teach me "how to take a soft shoulder," which he considered a necessary skill when narrow two-lane roads were the norm in Northern California.

Perhaps his love of driving is best exemplified by the many car trips he took south of the border. In 1934 he toured Mexico in a Model A Ford. In 1946 my parents did the same in a 1939 supercharged Graham-Paige. In the summer of 1956, my father and I did so in a 1953 Studebaker Commander, the model year famous for its sleek, Raymond Loewy design. The goal was a to take a new stretch of the Pan American Highway to the Mayan ruins at Chichén Itzá on the Yucatan peninsula. Before the journey began, my father decided to take a side trip to Banff, Canada. As I said, he loved to drive. As a consequence, we never made it as far south as Yucatan before summer's end and the start of the new school year.

During the trip I remember traveling through the vast emptiness of the Sonoran Desert one must cross to reach central Mexico. With no posted speed limit and no other car in sight, my father pushed the Studebaker to its limit of one hundred and five miles per hour. Upon cresting a small rise, we saw a dark object on the road ahead. We soon realized it was a vulture gorging itself on roadkill. In spite of my father's effort to slow the car, we bore down on the creature at an alarming rate. Startled by our sudden approach, the enormous bird began to flap its wings in a desperate attempt to get airborne. I had a horrific vision of it crashing through the windshield and decorating the interior of the car with its stinking innards. Fortunately, the Studebaker's front-sloping design created a slipstream which carried the bird safely over the top of the car, so no harm was done to us or the bird.

On long car trips my father insisted on early starts; therefore, it was only seven in the morning when we arrived in Ajijic (pronounced ah-hee´-heek) on the shores of Lake Chapala. In later years, Ajijic became a trendy artists' colony much like San Miguel de Allende. However, at the time it was just a sleepy Mexican village. A dozen chickens scattered before us as we entered town. Spotting an elderly man shambling along the cobblestone street, I asked him in my limited Spanish where my father and I could have breakfast. He pointed to a nearby hotel, the blank façade of which faced directly on the street. We entered the unnamed hotel through its weathered wooden door which had been left invitingly ajar. We found ourselves in an attractive, open-air lobby, the polished tile floor of which was graced with a number of potted palms. A metal cage stood in the corner, its sole occupant being a parrot which studied us with a cocked, yellow eye. My father approached the unoccupied registration desk and pinged the bell on the countertop. Receiving no response, we looked about the room and noticed an arched opening which we entered. To our surprise, we found ourselves in a forest of tall banana plants which had all the mystery and lushness of those jungle scenes painted by Rousseau. The overarching leaves created a tunnel in which small birds swooped back and forth, passing perilously close overhead. We descended a tiled path which led to a white, thatched-roofed cottage at the lake's edge. Its small dining room was furnished in colorful, handcrafted tables and chairs, and its window shutters were open to the lake, the damp, sweet-water scent of which filled the room. A young girl in pigtails emerged from the kitchen wearing a white *huipil* embroidered with red, yellow, and blue flowers.

She seated us at a window table in the otherwise empty restaurant and handed us menus. In my best high school Spanish, I ordered scrambled eggs with chorizo sausage, corn tortillas, glasses of orange juice, and a cup of dark-roasted coffee for my father and one of hot chocolate for me. There was something pleasingly different about the Mexican orange juice and hot chocolate, the former being less acidic that its North American counterpart and the latter being frothy with hints of cinnamon and vanilla.

At that early hour, the lake was veiled in a layer of mist through which a lone fisherman paddled a canoe, periodically pausing to dip his butterfly net into the water to catch the lake's prized white fish. The quiet was so profound I thought I could hear the lapping of the canoe's small wake as it gently broke upon the shore with the sound of silence.

As the years pass, my memory of that Mexican trip has faded, much like the color of my father's Kodak slides. But I have never forgotten that breakfast in Ajijic. I am told Lake Chapala is now polluted and the white fish long gone, so it is just as well I never returned. And I do not plan on doing so, having reached the age where the pain of travel exceeds its pleasures. I now find it easier to rely upon my memory. Recalling past events is like playing one of those tabletop jukeboxes from the nineteen fifties. Just press A56. Instead of hearing Fats Domino sing *Blueberry Hill,* suddenly it is 1956 and, to the sound of silence, I am having breakfast in Ajijic, where the orange juice is sweeter, the hot chocolate frothy, and a lone fisherman dips his butterfly net into the waters of Lake Chapala where the white fish are plentiful.

# Blessing of the Poet—*Yangtze River Fortune*

## *John Petraglia*

At dinner at the Yangtze River Café we open our fortunes.
Caroline begins, happily smashing her pale amber cookie.
*You have a unique sense of humor and love to laugh.*
We smile with her fortune's truth,
her loveliness and lack of pretense a rare, constant joy.

Ed reads his. *It is most enjoyable to listen to your stories.*
Now I wonder how these apt fortunes have found us here.
Ed recounts exploits we re-relish with his telling.
Like when we were counselors to juvenile delinquents
thirty years and thousands of miles ago
and young *Brother Droop*, whose talent was mimicking sirens
sounded his Paris Metropole alarm in stalled traffic
parting the streets en route to a Bronx halfway house.

Then mine. *You find beauty and wonder in ordinary things.*
I think to the time I asked Ed for a ride to work.
In sympathy, he says, "You drive this every morning?"
"Yes! The back roads of Lexington and Concord,
Carlisle's five-acre zoning, toppled-down stone walls,
ancient silver beeches I have come to know.
Each season bringing its wonder.

I think too of the coral roses I bought last year
whose petals I sent to Mary in a letter.
Later she told me when opening the envelope in her car
she did not notice petals falling to her lap,
nor realize they wafted the oriental spices
she imagined with her eager reading.

Or to this day how I so clearly remember Zulekha
taking off her glove the moment our hands first touched,
or spotting her copper-colored hair across a lobby,
barely contained in an azure tie.

I recall eating January oranges with my daughter.
How we laughed as sweet juices ran down our chins.
Nicole insists I'm doing it wrong and shows me how,
then stops mid slurp, "Wait, this is kind of a poem."
I watch her make notes on the back of a napkin,
warmed with another memory for our ages.

Caroline's laugh breaks my reverie.
Yes, I find beauty and wonder in ordinary things.
Yangtze River fortunes, lovely Caroline, Ed's stories,
sweet rose petal moments, orange eating, Zulekha!
all from a fortune cookie's inspiration.
Yes, I find beauty and wonder in simple things,
that is the insistent blessing of the poet.

# The Weight of Someone

## *Dana Rodney*

What I miss is the weight of someone. Another soul anchoring my space. The comfort of a solid, pulsing presence beside me as midnight exhales, and the coyotes howl in the field. Ten years have passed since I shared my life or home with anyone; children grown, men refused. I absurdly thought I could find the perfect man, and kept rejecting the specimens at hand, expecting something better. Now, nearing sixty, I am alone, and am aware it will remain that way. Not just because I am old and plump and gray, but because I have stopped making room for anyone. Alone is now the comfort zone. My brain has grudgingly made the adjustment.

How sad it is to admit defeat in the decades-long quest to find a soulmate. Sadder still to admit that were Mister Perfect to walk up to me today, I would no longer know what to do with him.

It is the weight of someone I miss. At times I go out to walk in the northern California dusk, and I hold my hands out to the horses in the fields. Sometimes they lay their heads on my back and the weight of it gladdens me. In the morning, waiting until I stir, my little dog climbs on my chest and spreads his small girth on me. It is his way of saying "Good Morning, I'm glad you're still here." The weight of him is nice and somewhat funny, and so I get up and fill his food bowl. This has become my intimate life.

In the mornings, after I feed the dog, I take my breakfast to the backyard to watch the hummingbirds. They weigh only as much as a penny. They have become the souls anchoring me, so lightly, that sometimes it feels like I am floating.

It is the weight of someone I miss. The weighty press of lips, the solid weight of another hand, of something to reach out and grasp. The counterbalance of body leaning into body. The depressions forming evenly on both sides of the bed, the weight of two dinner plates in my hand instead of one. But I've become used to it, the unsought emptiness of space around me, my body, and the planet's core creating a grudging relationship of gravity that is my only lasting companion.

# Ex

*Amber Lea Starfire*

I miss him sometimes
a bleached memory
after all these years
fading into the present
like a glimpse of ghost

I don't miss the arrogance
or crazy, misshapen sense
of random reality
his manic-depressive up-down
roller coaster

I miss his music
his bodacious audacity
to be authentic
a constant challenge to rise
to the moment

To be more than I think
I can be
the freedom of rhythm
the clash of chord
the beauty of melody

What I miss most of all
is waking to his long-fingered
piano, a heart full of longing
rising and falling
like a bird through the air

# Second Flight:
# Lighthearted

# Circus Act

## *Jan Flynn*

Scrambling in cowboy boots and short shorts over a cage full of tigers was not what I'd planned on doing, that morning in July of 1973. As summer jobs went, this one was turning out to be anything but boring.

I had been hired as a hostess at Marine World/Africa USA, back in the days when it was an amalgam of water shows and animal acts in a park dredged out of the sloughs of Redwood City, California, on land now occupied by the corporate headquarters of Oracle.

I was issued a hostess uniform: a blue-and-orange polyester tunic over matching shorts, the kind of shorts that were referred to at the time as "hot pants." The outfit provided me and the other hostesses scant protection from the chill winds that blew in off the bay, or from the glaring sun refracting off the water when the wind died down—guaranteeing that we would alternately freeze or roast. Still, it beat filing invoices or answering telephones in a dreary office, as I'd done in previous summers.

I reported each morning and was given one of a number of rotating assignments for the day: taking tickets at the front gate, babysitting the dolphin-petting pool, or managing the crowds at the killer whale show. Within a few weeks I got to know most of the park denizens, both animal and human. I hung out with the divers, the water-ski acrobats, the whale and dolphin trainers, the show announcers. I befriended the chimp wrangler and the elephant trainers.

One morning, before the gates opened, one of the big-cat handlers invited me to pet the mountain lion. I knelt beside the reclining feline, who regarded me with an expression of conditional tolerance. I gingerly stroked her luxurious fur while the trainer kept an eye out for park management. As long as the work got done and the crowds were kept happy, the park execs maintained an attitude of genial indifference toward their employees.

Among my new acquaintances was Fess Reynolds, a wizened gnome whose rich Texas drawl spun out story after story of his life as a cowboy and movie wrangler. He could, he assured me, boss anything with four feet. It wasn't an idle boast. He was the trainer for all the performing hoofed stock at the African Adventure show, including a murderous zebra whom nobody else dared approach, a juvenile giraffe with a custom-built saddle, Taco the llama, Frosty the Brahma bull, Sarge the water buffalo, and Sheila, the park's famous kissing camel. Fess took a shine to me because I was a rapt audience for his yarns, and at some point I told him I rode horses—which was true—although I may have elaborated as to the extent of my skills.

African Adventure had its own dedicated cast of handlers and trainers, but Fess needed an extra rider to fill out the schedule. I was thrilled when he asked.

From that point on, three days a week, I interrupted my hostess duties to head backstage where I donned items from Fess's own wardrobe: a spangled western shirt, a cowboy hat, and ostrich-leather cowboy boots that fit me surprisingly well. I still wore the blue and orange hot pants.

The show took place in a large outdoor amphitheater. The backstage area, a warren of enclosures and cages that contained everything from Margie the elephant to a bloody-minded harpy eagle, was concealed from the audience by screens and backdrops. A platoon of stagehands would set up a series of tunnel cages that ran from backstage into a huge, collapsible enclosure placed center stage for the lion and tiger acts. The instant the big cats were finished, the crew had to stow the whole contraption to make way for the rest of the program. This required some distraction for the audience, and this is where I came in.

My job was to ride Sarge the water buffalo in the "Balancing Act." As the cat cages were rolled away, two stagehands dragged a gigantic seesaw into the center of the amphitheater. Fess would ride out on the giraffe while a young woman, a professional rider, would trot up astride Sheila the camel. Both strode around the arena before guiding their mounts to step onto either end of the seesaw. At that point, I would lumber out atop Sarge, urge him up onto to the fulcrum point, and walk him forwards and backwards. This caused the seesaw go up and down, raising and lowering by turns the camel and the giraffe. The audience, puzzled, applauded tepidly as we raised our hats in a salute before relinquishing the stage to the bird wrangler with his trained hawk and eagle.

In the finale, I rode Frosty the Brahma bull in a parade consisting of all the less dangerous animals, festooned in whatever way possible with American flags.

I didn't mention any of this to my parents. It was like running away with the circus, except without leaving home.

What could go wrong? Frosty was patient and sweet-tempered, while Sarge was docile to the point of lethargy. Fess outfitted my boots with rowel spurs that looked like they could disembowel a horse, and showed me the nails that were embedded lengthwise, pointy end out, in the ends of the thick rope reins that were part of both Frosty's and Sarge's tack.

"Use 'em, but don't let the audience see 'em" Fess said. The park touted its policy of "Affection Training" in its marketing.

Frosty never gave me any trouble, responding to my clucks and encouragement. Sarge, whose hide was tougher than a Samsonite, was not so amenable. When the mood to stand still came upon him, the spurs and nail points made no impression. Once Sarge developed a habit of balking on me, it grew worse. One day he refused to move offstage no matter what I did. The giraffe and camel had made their exits long seconds before, and there I sat atop Sarge with a fixed smile on my face, surreptitiously kicking at his flanks and poking his withers. At length a stagehand ran out with a cattle prod and touched it to Sarge's backside. The effect was remarkable. Sarge snorted and seemed to levitate, then rumbled straight backstage at a brisk trot, a pace I hadn't thought him capable of. From then on, all I had to do to get him moving was to touch him with the end of a rein while uttering a low "Zzzzt."

One day I arrived backstage to find more than the usual amount of pre-show tumult. The young woman who rode the camel hadn't shown up, due to a domestic disturbance at home. It wasn't clear who was in jail, she or her husband. As I pulled on my boots, Fess, wearing a grim look, stalked up to me.

"Honey, you're gonna have to ride that camel," he said.

I blinked at him. Not only was Sheila enormous and high-strung, she was at that moment in her stable, on the opposite side of the tunnel cages holding the tigers awaiting the opening of the show. Fess handed me a long, crop-style whip. "You climb on over those cages and go get on Sheila. Go on now," he directed, and such was the force of his command that I complied.

Fueled by adrenaline, I clambered up, over, and down the chain-link enclosure, aware of the fascinated stares of the tigers. My pantyhose snagged and tore as I jumped down the last couple of feet. Ripping away the last few strands, I ran toward the stagehand who held the camel in position, hunkered down on her haunches. I hoisted myself into the saddle, grabbed the reins, and repositioned the crop in my sweating palm.

The opening music swelled. Sheila bawled in anticipation.

"You ready?" asked the stagehand, looking dubious.

I nodded, he let go of the reins, and Sheila lurched to her feet.

The music blared a fanfare, Sheila's cue. I'd had a split second to discover how very tall a camel is when you're sitting on it, and how very remote its head is, out there at the end of reins that look ten feet long, when she broke into a rolling lope, heading into the arena. I smiled for the audience, feeling as though I were in the crow's nest of a ship battling high seas.

Fess, astride the giraffe, met us at the apex of the arena. "Make her bow, honey. Tap her on the left shoulder and tell her 'Cush'!" he urged, his voice pitched to reach me below the music and the crowd's laughter.

"Cush, Sheila!" I said, whapping at whatever shoulder I could reach. She seemed to consider my request, but the music changed to her exit cue. She performed a sudden about-face and launched off toward backstage at top speed. I clung on, ducking roof beams as she skidded around cages until she reached her own stall. Coming to an abrupt halt, Sheila instantly forgot the previous five minutes. She peered with delicate interest into her feed bin.

"CUSH, Sheila!" I said, landing the crop squarely on the correct shoulder this time. She crumpled obediently to the ground. I dismounted, wobbly-legged. A stagehand walked me out of her stall.

Fess appeared, red-faced, the strain of his staffing crisis rippling visibly through his tiny frame. "Go get Taco, now!" he ordered. "You gotta ride that llama next. Go on, now, GO!"

With that, he darted into the chaos backstage.

I stared after him. The llama was a beautiful animal, but only two people ever handled him—Fess and the rider who was currently AWOL. Taco held strong opinions. When annoyed, he would pin his ears back and eject a stream of stinking cud straight at the offending party.

The stagehands usually gave Taco a wide berth due to the cud issue, but they were more afraid of Fess. The guy wrangling me grabbed my arm and thrust me into a dark stall where Taco, tethered by his lead to a post, regarded me suspiciously. "Just unhook his lead, snap it to his halter, and get up on him," instructed the stagehand. "Hurry up!"

I ducked under Taco's head, hoping to stay out of cud-firing range, and fumbled at the clasp that attached him to the post. The music swelled towards the entrance cue; shaky with nerves, I looked for help from the stagehand, but he too had disappeared. I took a deep breath, unhooked the clasp, and snapped it next to the other end beneath Taco's muzzle. This, I would later discover, was a mistake.

I led the llama into the passageway. He followed—with an air of reserving judgment, in case this was some sort of emergency—but as I struggled to get on him, he pinned his ears further and further back. He wore neither saddle nor bareback pad. His fur was long, luxuriant, and slippery, and his back stood at a level somewhere above my waist. It was no help that I was still wearing what was left of my panty hose and, of course, those spurs. I threw myself belly-first onto his back, and crawled around until I had one leg on either side of his flanks.

Taco was already moving toward the arena, no doubt in an effort to get away from me rather than out of a desire to perform. As we reached the view of the audience, I'd gotten a grip on the reins and was sitting up straight, but the now-furious llama was determined to offload me.

He advanced in a series of stiff-legged hops. After every four or five hops, he would halt and plunge his head toward the ground in a determined effort to dislodge me. I hung on, thankful that he was both anatomically incapable of bucking, and too preoccupied to spit cud at the audience.

We lurched toward the apex of the arena, again to be met by Fess, this time riding the zebra. Sizing up the situation, he muttered, "Turn him around at the cue, and go get Frosty."

The music changed. I pulled with the left rein to guide Taco backstage, but since I had both ends of the reins snapped under his muzzle rather than at either side, I lacked directional control. Moreover, Taco had by now lost all patience with me. He clearly intended to stay right where he was, downstage center, hopping and heaving. Fess and the zebra, meanwhile, had trotted offstage, leaving me to draw the whoops and cackles of the audience.

In desperation, I reached beneath Taco's chin and hauled to the left with both reins while giving him a hearty slap with my knees. Surprised, he straightened up and trotted homewards, only stopping twice to try and dump me. I ignored the catcalls and the super-eight movie cameras aimed in my direction.

Backstage, I slid off the llama's back, both of us ready to call a truce. Recovering my breath, I headed toward good old reliable Frosty.

"Never mind Frosty! Go get Sheila again!" roared Fess, who had materialized at my side. "You gotta ride Sheila in the finale!" he shrieked, and was off again. Evidently Sheila's star power meant that Frosty was getting bumped from his place in the curtain call.

At least this time there were no tiger cages to climb over. Clambering aboard the camel once again, I took the reins, feeling almost confident. I cooed reassuringly at Sheila. The music swelled toward the cue for the finale.

Just before the camel rose to her feet, a stagehand ran up with an American flag on a three-foot pole. "Got your flag," he informed me.

"My what?" I asked, as he shoved the pole into my left boot, and Sheila rocked herself to a standing position. I had forgotten that this was the July 4th weekend. I reached to adjust the flagpole digging into my ankle, just as Sheila heard her cue and flung her gigantic mass into a lope.

We hove into view of the audience. A stiff breeze caught the flag and blew it over my face.

The fabric flapping against my head failed to muffle the gasps and laughter of the audience. I grabbed the reins in my right hand and used my left to dig the flag out of my boot, holding it aloft. I remained astride as Sheila and I took our place behind Margie the elephant. The parade was blessedly brief.

Once backstage, dismounted and on terra firma, I paused to regain my breath. I felt about two feet tall and had a queasy sense of motion, although I was standing still. It dawned on me what I had just done.

I couldn't wait to do it again.

# Wine in a Bucket

## *Bo Kearns*

Norman lived alone in a white bungalow on Elm Street in Napa, California. Like others of his generation, the retired schoolteacher had a "bucket list." Though he dreamed of climbing Mt. Kilimanjaro or seeing the Taj Mahal, he lived on Social Security and a small pension. By necessity, his list was local.

On Norman's seventieth birthday, he splurged on a bottle of vintage cabernet sauvignon. He retrieved one of the two Riedel crystal goblets in the cupboard and wiped off the dust. They had last been used as a pair in celebration of his fiftieth wedding anniversary. But after Dolores passed away a few years ago, there hadn't been much to celebrate. He extracted the cork, poured a small amount and held the glass to the light. He admired the deep, rich, red color and smiled. He swirled the wine and sniffed the bouquet. He savored a sip and quietly said, "Happy Birthday, Norman."

As he did on every birthday, Norman got his bucket list from the desk drawer. Over time he had managed to cross out several items. He stared at one still there: *Attend Napa Valley Wine Auction.* He leaned back in his chair and pictured himself mingling among the rich and famous while sipping Napa's finest. He sighed and shook himself back to reality. The cost of a ticket was well beyond his means. Still, he held out hope.

Days later, as he sat at the kitchen table reading the newspaper, an article caught his eye—"Wine auction seeks volunteers." He scanned the list of opportunities: "Parking attendant, Limo driver, Crew cleanup," etc. Nothing appealed until he spotted "Assist in the barrel room." His pulse quickened. The barrel room would be the scene of the action. He visualized himself standing with the winemakers, talking about terroir, while surrounded by frenzied bidders in designer pastels raising their paddles on high.

He hastened to the computer and filled out the online application. That night he tossed in his sleep, worried he might not get accepted. No need to feel anxious. The following day he received an email, "Welcome, Volunteer Norman."

The day of the auction, Norman arrived early and joined the other volunteers gathering at the staging area. The men wore the prescribed khaki pants and white shirts, the women sported navy skirts and white blouses. When the shuttle bus pulled up, they all piled on. Norman sat in the back. He gazed around, noticing how much younger everyone else looked. Lately, that had been the trend no matter where he went, yet it didn't bother him. He found their high energy contagious. The bus lumbered along Highway 29 past rows of lush vines, the June grape clusters still a pale green. He eavesdropped on the conversations of those around him. It seemed that most worked for wineries.

"Our winemaker made a rosé this year. Bad move," said a woman with long red hair.

"He should have stuck to cabs and chardonnay," replied the man seated beside her.

"How's business?" someone else inquired.

"Better than last year," came the reply. A nod of heads provided group confirmation. Norman took a deep breath and smiled. He had managed to maneuver his way into the wine business and was now headed to the biggest event of the season.

The bus pulled up to an old, three-story stone building thick with ivy. The volunteers filed off and headed for the registration table. A bespectacled gray-haired woman located Norman's nametag and handed him a long beige apron with the auction logo emblazoned across the front. "Yours to keep," she said. Norman beamed. He hadn't counted on a gift.

"Report downstairs to the barrel room," the woman said. "Look for Holly. She's your team leader. She'll tell you what to do."

Norman weaved his way through the crowd and down the winding staircase to a cavernous room where massive oak barrels lined the rock walls. The sun's rays filtered through the small windows high above, casting a hazy aura over the scene. The air had a pleasant chill. Norman paused to bask in the heady atmosphere.

A young woman in a black cocktail dress, fishnet stockings, and high heels stood in the middle of the room. Surrounded by a sea of khaki pants and navy skirts, she held a clipboard with a sheaf of papers. Must be Holly, Norman thought, suspecting that honchos got to wear whatever they wanted.

As he joined the group, he heard Holly say to a couple, "You two will be covering Blackbird and Shafer." Norman recognized the names as two of the most respected wineries in the Valley. He could hardly wait to find out where he would be stationed.

The next volunteer stepped forward. "Are you sure you registered?" Holly asked as she scanned her list.

"Positive," the man replied. She looked skeptical and checked again.

"I really don't have time to deal with you right now," Holly said, her brow furrowed. "Chill for a while. I'll see if I can find something for you to do upstairs."

She turned her attention to Norman.

"Name's Norman Norman," he said pointing to his tag.

Holly's eyes flashed. "Hardly amusing. You're holding up the line."

Norman hadn't expected to encounter Nurse Ratched at the wine auction. Tempted to tell her to check her attitude at the door, he kept his cool. He didn't want to risk getting booted upstairs.

"Norman Norman's my name," he said. "My parents were from the Midwest. They liked everything simple, even their children." Holly shook her head.

"Looks like Opus One for you, Norman Norman." Norman pumped his fist. He had arrived at the pinnacle of wine snobbery.

"Don't get so excited," Holly said. "Your job is emptying the spit buckets."

Norman froze. Surely, he had misheard.

"Make sure there's no overflow," Holly continued. "Wouldn't want our guests to slip and fall."

Before Norman could protest, Holly cut him off.

"Do a good job and next year you'll get to work one of the bid tables." Holly glanced over his shoulder. "Next."

Norman slunk away. He considered sneaking out the back door, but he had committed. At least he wouldn't have to worry about seeing anyone he knew. Those attending lived in a rarefied world of private jets, villas, and Monet originals on the wall.

Around the room, winemakers stood beside their barrels, busy drawing wine from a bunghole. Tasters swirled the liquid in their mouths. They considered the taste. Then they spat into a silver bucket on the table. Norman stood by watching. He remembered Holly's admonition about overflow. Sensing the moment, he grabbed the handles and lifted, while hoping he wouldn't pinch a nerve in his neck. He made his way through the crowd toward the consolidation vat in the corner. He had to be fast. Someone might want to expectorate before he returned.

After several trips, Norman paused to catch his breath. There has to be a better way, he thought. He searched in the storage room and discovered several more large vats. He took them out and placed them strategically around the room. Now, with less travel time, there was no need for so many runners. Norman had worked himself out of a job. Proud of his initiative, he felt entitled to stroll about, sip wine, and pretend to be one of them. But he had to be careful to avoid Holly.

As he strolled past the Frank Family Cellars table, he noticed a long line of irritated bidders. An attractive woman, her short, dark hair streaked with gray, sat squinting, looking harried as she tried to process bids.

"Can I help?" Norman asked.

"Oh, please," she said. "Holly assigned me to the most popular station. I should have told her I'm dyslexic. I have processing problems."

Norman assessed the situation. As she recorded bids in the ledger, someone needed to update the large bid board on the wall behind her. He seized the moment and mounted the ladder. "I'll take care of the board; you do the rest," he said.

The bidding kicked into high gear. The price for a case of wine accelerated. How terrific! What a great day for Napa, Norman thought. All that money goes to local charities.

"You're doing a great job, Norman," the winemaker called up to him. "When you have time, come down and taste some wine."

About to accept, Norman spotted Holly approaching. He scrunched down, hoping she wouldn't see him.

"Norman, what are you doing up there? You're supposed to be emptying spit buckets." Her hands on her hips, she stood and glared.

"Everything's under control," Norman replied. "Check for yourself."

"Norman's a big help. I couldn't do this on my own. Don't take him away," the dyslexic woman pleaded. Norman suspected that even hardened Holly would be unable to refuse a woman seeking help.

Holly turned and walked off, her high heels clicking in staccato.

Suddenly the ladder beneath Norman shook. The room resonated with the rattle of glasses and crashing objects. Earthquake!

With fear in her eyes, the dyslexic woman clutched the table.

Norman jumped down to console her. "Just a tremor," he said, though sounding unsure.

"Everyone, keep calm," came the voice over the loudspeaker. "Welcome to California. Just our usual shaking." The crowd returned to drinking. Norman, about to remount the ladder, felt another, much stronger tremor. And he heard a loud rumble, like that of a freight train gaining speed. He glanced toward the main aisle, and saw a dislodged barrel headed straight for a tall man, busy texting on his cellphone. Norman sprang into action.

He bolted across the room, and with memories of his former days on the gridiron, he lowered his shoulder, lunged forward, and knocked the man off his feet. The pair sprawled across the floor.

"What the hell?" the man yelled, his arms flailing. Norman scrambled to his feet and helped him up. At the far end, the barrel hit the wall and exploded like a hard-hit piñata. Wine shot into the air and a tide of red spread across the floor. The man, still grasping his cell phone, turned to Norman. "You saved my life," he said. Norman recognized him. He was the owner of the Golden State Warriors, San Francisco's beloved basketball champions. The owner took a card from his wallet and handed it to Norman. "Call my secretary. She'll arrange for season tickets for two."

Norman stared at the card in the familiar royal-blue-and-gold colors. He hadn't done anything special. About to protest, Norman looked up to see that the owner had moved on. Too bad Dolores wasn't still alive, Norman thought. She loved basketball. He wondered whom he'd ask to go with him. He turned his attention back to the far end. The scene resembled a war zone. People milled about in shock. Norman grabbed cloths off the tables to wipe up the spill. "You'll be okay," he assured a woman, her yellow dress covered with red blotches. When there was nothing more he could do, he returned to his station.

"You're a hero," the dyslexic woman exclaimed while giving him a hug. He realized he didn't know her name. He glanced at her tag: "Rose," his favorite flower.

"Rose, do you like basketball?"

"I'm not sure. My ex-husband would never take me to a game. He said I wouldn't be able to follow the fast action."

"Don't worry. I'll explain it," Norman said.

At the end of the long day, Norman returned home. He opened a bottle of cabernet sauvignon, a thank-you gift from an event winemaker. He poured a glass and held it up to the light. He admired the deep red color. He swirled, sniffed, and sipped. He detected flavors of ripe plum and blackberry with hints of vanilla and cocoa. He wondered what kind of wine Rose liked. He suspected a crisp sauvignon blanc.

Norman took his bucket list from the desk drawer. He smiled as he crossed through *Attend Napa Valley Wine Auction.* Further down, he crossed out: *Get tickets to see a Warriors game* and *Find a girlfriend.*

# Hard-boiled

### *Barbara Toboni*

While in college I worked
in the composing department
of our local newspaper
One day my boss, the editor-in-chief,
zipped past my desk on his harried way
to the paste-up tables
He glanced in my direction
and blurted out
You think too hard
I had paused the slow tapping of the keys
on my headline machine
to consider the next banner
POLICE NEED HELP FINDING
HIT-AND-RUN DRIVER

I lit a cigarette and watched as smoke
swirled above my head
*You think too hard*
What did he mean?
Insult or compliment?
I puffed as I considered
and I have considered it ever since

I have come to a conclusion
The remark was not an insult
although his tone seemed abrupt
and it could not have been a compliment
A compliment would sound more like
*I like your way of thinking*

Therefore *You think too hard*
was a hard-boiled observation
Although now I'm enjoying
the remark as a compliment
What kind of poet would I be
if I didn't think too hard?

# The Queen of Tonga

*Aletheia Morden*

I was watching Queen Elizabeth's coronation on our new television in June of 1953 when my father's relatives arrived, clumping up the stairs to our flat in my grandmother's Edwardian house. They were hours late. They'd missed seeing Princess Margaret riding in the glass coach, which wasn't made of glass at all. It was painted black and blue with a lot of gilt trim and big windows so the crowds could get a good view of the Queen Mother wearing the Koh-i-Noor Diamond in her crown, one of the largest diamonds in the world. They'd missed the entire procession to Westminster Abbey through the streets of London where British Commonwealth soldiers, wearing their World War II medals, lined the route. Palace guards were wearing their beaver helmets and policemen their capes because it was a cold and rainy summer's day.

Most importantly, they'd missed seeing the Queen riding in the Gold State Coach with its carved and gilded mythical sea gods blowing conch shells—its dolphins and cherubs, the lion's head, and a sculpted crown on top—all pulled by eight Windsor Grey horses. I held a miniature souvenir of it in my seven-year-old hands, a fragile surprise gift from one of my mother's relatives, Aunt Bunny (whose real name was Elsa, but the British middle and upper classes used stupid nicknames in those days).

Ten minutes' oration on the state of the weather went on behind me as the relatives struggled out of their wet coats and hats. They'd missed seeing the Queen enter the Abbey with her pages and ladies-in-waiting flanked by a long row of her personal guards on each side, white plumes on their steel helmets swaying in time as they slowly marched in their high black boots down the long aisle towards the altar, drawn swords pointed down by their sides. The relatives had also missed the news reporters' description of the ceremony, which dated from 974 A.D., and was now being conducted in English rather than Latin for the modern, worldwide television audience of 277 million people. They'd also missed news tidbits such as the success of Edmund Hillary and his Sherpa guide, Tenzing Norgay, in being the first to reach the summit of Mount Everest—New Zealand's gift to the new queen. Meanwhile, over on the Korean peninsula, we were told that Canadian soldiers serving in the Korean war had libated the occasion with special rum rations and fired red, white, and blue smoke shells at the enemy.

"What've we missed?" Great Aunt Mary asked, seating herself in one of the chairs arranged in a semicircle in front of the nine-inch black-and-white screen.

"Nothing much," my father replied, struggling with an armload of hats and coats. "It's on all day. Sit on the floor," he said to me. "Aunt Margaret needs that armchair."

I moved as directed, sitting cross-legged about twelve inches from the TV.

"Move!" Grandpa Albert and Uncle Stan roared in unison. "We can't see!"

"Come and sit on the floor by us," Aunt Margaret said. She had my four-year-old cousin on her lap—spoilt Christine—who spied the little gold coach in my hand and wanted to play with it. I ignored her.

"Don't be so selfish," Grandmother Winifred admonished me. "Share."

Spoit Christine made a grab for my new toy with her chubby little paws and promptly broke it.

I was heartbroken; I didn't have many toys. At school, I'd drawn a charcoal picture of the coach that had pleased me. I'd planned to add it to my own personal art gallery on the wooden walls of my playhouse, formerly known as my late maternal grandfather's photographic studio, also known as the garden shed. My teacher had had other ideas; she'd entered it into our town's exhibit of Coronation Art, and I'd never seen it again.

"Go in your bedroom if you want to cry," my father ordered. "We're watching this." He had his eyes glued to the television screen, as did his relatives, now that they'd taken their seats. None of them had a television. My maternal grandmother had retreated to her son's house for a few days, where the screen was larger and the armchairs more comfortable.

"I've put the kettle on," my mother announced. And so began the ritual of endless cups of tea and slices of my mother's fruit cake: tea so strong I was sure it would burn holes in the flowered chintz-covered armchair if you spilled a drop; iced fruitcake that did who-knows-what horrors to your intestinal tract.

Food had been rationed during World War II and for several years following. Dried fruit had come off ration in 1951, tea in 1952, and eggs in 1953. Sugar was in the process of coming off ration, so today's fruitcake was a special treat. My mother had cut out little black-and-white head shots of the Royal family from the newspaper, and propped them on the icing: Queen Elizabeth; her constantly complaining husband, Prince Philip; and the two Royal children, Charles and Ann, sat in a sticky row. Perhaps my mother thought they mirrored her own family, since she always thought of herself as a princess—and we had added my brother six months earlier, making us a family of four. She and the Queen were born around the same time and almost shared the same name: Elizabeth and Betty. And—final proof—my mother was fond of pointing to the veins in her wrist and declaring: "Look, blue blood." Or perhaps, as she told me decades later, married life was so boring to her after the excitement of being young and in uniform during World War II, my mother lived a parallel life to save her sanity.

With everyone's eyes on the televised ceremony as they sipped their first cup of tea—my mother had planned the fruitcake cutting for after the crown was placed on the Queen's head—spoilt

Christine grew bored and restless. She wasn't interested in my baby brother, who lay in his pram sucking a pacifier dipped in sugar and watching everything going on around him.

"Why don't you both go outside and play in the garden," my mother suggested, looking out the window. "It's stopped raining."

"I want to watch this," I protested. My objections fell on deaf ears. Spoilt Christine liked the idea of playing in the garden, and the relatives liked the idea of not having to listen to her whining.

I was disappointed, but made the best of the afternoon while fuming internally at my little cousin. We played snail races along the garden path, after rounding up every garden snail we could find from the lawn and vegetable plot. We played chase in and out of my grandmother's fruit bushes—until one of the snails got squashed underfoot, and we had to conduct a burial service. Scooping out a shallow depression in the dirt, I nudged the unlucky snail into the hole with the toe of my shoe, dropped in a few blades of grass; then, using the side of my shoe, covered the grave with soil while singing the children's hymn, "All Things Bright and Beautiful."

When we started playing hide and seek, I sneaked back indoors when it was my time to hide. I'd done enough of my duty for the day.

On the television, Queen Elizabeth had been anointed by the Archbishop of Canterbury and was being crowned. A discussion about crown size was in progress amongst the relatives as the camera panned the Abbey audience—the women's were considerably smaller than the men's, Aunt Margaret noted. Men's crowns sat securely on their heads; the women's petite crowns perched on top of their heads, "looking as though, if a woman put a foot down wrong, her crown would fall off," Grandma Winifred surmised. My father maintained that the women wore smaller crowns because they had smaller brains. All the male relatives snickered, causing my mother to retort that since my father didn't have a brain at all, he wasn't qualified to say anything. Great-Aunt Mary settled it by saying that a lady's crown was smaller because it had to fit inside her tiara.

When spoilt Christine finally found me once more—plunked down cross-legged on the floor in front of the screen—she started complaining that it was her turn to hide; the relatives insisted we go back outside.

"Can't we stay and play with the baby?" I suggested hopefully.

My mother shook her head. "No. We don't want to disturb him while he's being good."

Resigned to missing most of the coronation that day, I sighed and went back to the garden, my cousin trailing behind me. We played ring-around-the-rosy for a while, and then spoilt Christine made a beeline for my playhouse, aka the garden shed. I barred the door.

"You're not worthy," I told her. She tried to push past me. I resisted. The time had come to make a deal.

"You can go in there if you let me go back in to watch television," I bargained.

She considered this for a moment, then pushed past me and tried to open the door.

"It's locked," I told her. "You need the magic key to get in there, but first you have to swear allegiance to a higher power. And let me go back inside and watch the coronation," I quickly added.

She stared at me with resentment, trying to understand what I meant, then capitulated. "Okay," she whined.

I retrieved the key with much ceremony from under a brick by the door and unlocked my playhouse. Then I quickly ran back to the television. A quick glance at the tea table showed that the cake was gone. I'd missed it! Not a crumb was left on the cake plate! The relatives had eaten it all.

I'd also missed some of the procession from the Abbey to Buckingham Palace: Queen Elizabeth II in her golden coach, Prime Minister Winston Churchill, and some of the 129 monarchs and heads of state in their carriages, now hooded, because the rain had become a downpour in London. Our television may have only shown black and white, but the reporter described the scene in color for my eager eyes and ears. Roars of applause rose from the crowd as Canadian Mounties in red uniforms rode by on their horses; loud cheers erupted as Scottish bagpipers marched along in their kilts— and as two of four military bands playing the Australian National Anthem ("Waltzing Matilda"), and the Victorian marching song ("Soldiers of the Queen"), paraded down the Mall.

But the loudest cheers of all were for the Queen of Tonga, a monarch nobody had ever seen before, riding in the rain with her carriage top down "so the people can see me and I can see them," as she told the newspapers. And the people loved her for it. Majestic Queen Salote Tupou III, six feet three inches tall and weighing three hundred pounds, laughed at the rain as she waved to the crowds. The Queen of Tonga, the only other female monarch in the British Commonwealth, became the unofficial star attraction that day, wearing her crimson-and-gold gown covered with the silk mantle of a Dame Grand Cross of the Order of the British Empire, and a tall red plume rising straight up in the air from her golden crown. She stayed almost dry, while her carriage mate, the Sultan of Kelantan, got soaked. Queen Salote became a British favorite. Baby girls born that month were christened Charlotte (the English form of the Polynesian Salote); a racehorse was named after her; and more than one song was written about her, including "Linger Longer, Queen of Tonga."

The cheering crowds for Queen Salote almost drowned out the screams of spoilt Christine as she ran down the garden path from my playhouse. Her father went out to rescue her. It turned out that my art gallery had terrified my cousin. Specifically, bright-colored crayon drawings of smiling relatives with very big teeth had proved just too scary for her, as they loomed over her from the wall.

Not my fault.

I turned back to the television, while the relatives fussed over Christine. My mother, stifling her laughter, whispered in my ear, "I saved you a piece of cake. You can have it after they all go home. It won't be long now."

# The Shopping Trip

### *Sarita Lopez*

"God dammit, try and find you-know-what! And hurry!" Jerry Everland heard the desperation in his wife's voice and scowled. He knew the goal and he knew what they had come for, but did Sherise need to speak so loudly? The woman had always had a voice that closely mimicked a foghorn, and today it seemed especially deafening. He gave himself a few precious seconds to mentally curse before taking a deep breath. He looked to his left, then his right, but instinct told him to go straight. Jerry began to sprint, hoping his New Balances lived up to their soft-soled reputation.

Each aisle was more demolished than the next, and signs that read "Containers," "Kitchenware," and "Beverages" swung dangerously from torn metal chains. Jerry would never be mistaken for a gym rat, and his beating heart pounded deep inside his chest, punishing him for not using his once-active Planet Fitness membership. He heard a grunting from nearby, and frantically turned right to duck into what looked like it had once been the baking aisle. He willed his breath to slow, waiting to see if he had been followed. As his eyes adjusted to the shitty lighting, his gaze fell upon a half-smashed bucket of lard and a single box of cupcake mix with Disney's latest Princess darling, Elsa, smiling invitingly as if calories didn't matter if you were under ten.

Telling himself nobody was coming, and that he was justified in needing a snack to keep his blood sugar from dipping, he reached for the cupcake mix, his mouth salivating at the thought of snowflake-shaped sprinkles. His hand wrapped around the cardboard box, his chubby fingers already picking at the top. Before he could revel in victory, a snarl behind him made the hair on the back of his neck stand to full attention. He whipped around, the Elsa-sponsored product in hand, his heart racing yet again at an uncomfortable speed.

Jerry stared down at what must have once been an attractive woman. With her light-pink cardigan (most likely from the local Chico's) and stained khaki slacks, she could have been a Catholic-school teacher. She was glaring at him. She crouched into a fighting position and hissed, her glassy gaze never leaving the sugary goodness in his hand. A shopping basket hung in the crook of her elbow. Inside the basket, turkey meat, an iPad and an issue of *People* magazine swayed as the woman swung her arm toward Jerry.

"Oh, *hell* no!" A flash of blonde fell onto the snarler. His wife! Sherise swung her fists, connecting with the maybe teacher's throat, who gasped for air but stood her ground. The young woman's eyes shifted between Jerry's small prize and Sherise, perhaps deciding who would be the easiest target. Sherise moved first, leaping onto the woman's back and letting out a blood-curdling scream. They both fell to the ground, spit flying, clumps of hair ripping out of scalps. The pain only seemed to amplify their anger, and their fight became even more violent.

Jerry watched in sick perversion. Nothing about the day had gone smoothly. He would have been completely fine not going outside today, but Sherise had insisted. After twelve years of marriage, Jerry knew it was best to adhere to the words embroidered on one of their sofa's cushions—"Happy Wife, Happy Life." He had sighed, and hemmed and hawed, but they both knew he would give in, no matter what the outcome of the day would be.

When they first opened their front door, the moon had seemed just a bit too bright. They had rushed to their car and slowly backed out to avoid unwanted attention. The drive used to take five minutes. On a day like today, driving 20 miles per hour, it had taken almost thirty.

The parking lot was a nightmare—a sign of what they would find inside. Tipped-over shopping carts littered the pavement, while plastic bags floated lazily between ground and air. Abandoned cars cluttered walkways, some with the doors wide open. Jerry had shivered, wondering who would be in that much of a hurry that they wouldn't even close a door. He pulled their Subaru onto the sidewalk, right in front of a fire hydrant. The rules of where you could and could not park, at the moment, did not exist.

Before entering the store, Sherise grabbed Jerry's hands, and she gave a quick prayer. Then she grabbed her mace, nodded bravely at Jerry, and they both flung open their car doors—running for who knew what lay waiting for them inside.

They had been in the store for mere minutes before his wife was brawling on the floor like a schoolyard bully. Sherise took a punch to the face and howled in rage. Jerry made a move to help.

"I'm fine; just get the frickin car!"

He hesitated as another blow connected with Sherise's cheekbone.

"Go, baby, GO!"

Jerry ran, not looking back. Dripping sweat, his chest heaved and his gut swayed side to side as he looked for the right aisle.

Just as he thought he couldn't go any further, he turned and saw the toy section. His gaze fell on a mini Range Rover with sparkly pink paint—for kids ages two to five—marked fifty percent off. He only had one last burst of energy in him, and he rushed forward, grabbing the car and hugging it tightly. As the steering wheel ate into his chest, Jerry felt the same pride and relief he felt when his daughter, Savannah, was born.

"Oh baby, you did it!" Sherise limped toward him, her bruised eyes filling with tears.

"No, *we* did it."

They held each other, grinning broadly at the Range Rover. This is what they had come for, and while Sherise might have to take ibuprofen for the next week, it was worth it. It always was.

The intercom squeaked above. The store stood still.

"Er, your friendly team at Walmart wants to remind you that our Black Friday specials end at noon. And to the owner of the white Prius, you left your kid in her car seat. And your lights are on."

Jerry and Sherise got in line with the other victors. After their four-year-old daughter had informed them that all of her friends had mini-cars, and she would be "so so so *soooo* mad" if they didn't get her one for her upcoming December birthday, they knew they would have to brave the hells of discount holiday shopping to get their miracle baby what she wanted. The early morning's shopping yield was worth every rising welt and split lip.

A man two places ahead of them scratched at his semi-ripped-off toupee and gave a little laugh. "I always say I'm not going to shop this dang early, but a flat-screen TV for less than two hundred bucks? That's worth the no sleep!"

Others began to chime in, each showing off their carts and wounds like medals.

Jerry and Sherise were silent. It wasn't the first time they had experienced a midnight like this, and they knew it wouldn't be their last.

They'd be back next year.

Or possibly, and most likely, on Christmas Eve.

# No More Dead Men

## *Lisa Gibson*

No more dead men in my bed.
I lie awake inside my head.
It spins and churns and wonders why
my dead husband sleeps nearby.

I wonder, worry, ponder. FIE!

He chose to be the living dead
and take up space upon my bed.
I have no one to blame but me.
For I have let it be, and be, and
be, and be. I could go on.
But I have acquiesced too long.

I long for joy and love that's treasured,
but find the conversation measured.
Convoluted, twisted, bound,
angry shouting. Repeat round.

There is no reason not to kill
a man who cowardly lies still.
So if he likes to feign he's dead,
while taking space upon your bed.

Listen well and learn from teacher.
You'll want to have an extra freezer.
A Sawzall, tarp and tape are handy.
Smart girls keep a well-stocked pantry.

Then saunter sexy into Ace
your trademark smile upon your face.
Politely ask to speak to Herman.
His specialty;  removing vermin.

He limps and has a lazy eye.
His breath, roast beef and swiss on rye.
Poison? Yes. Machete?? Nope
Perhaps a yard or two of rope?

He hooks you up with what you need
then rings you up in lightning speed.
It's guaranteed though nothing's said.
No more dead men in your bed.

# The Frogman Cometh

*Aletheia Morden*

In 1968 I lived with my lover, Roy, above the Santa Monica Pier merry-go-round in an apartment he had rented for $12.00 a week from Mrs. Winslow, the pier manager. There were three rooms: a main room, a kitchen, and a bathroom. Roy took the kitchen door off its hinges and propped milk crates under each end so we could use it as a dining table.

One night we hosted a dinner party. Spaghetti served as the main course, washed down with a half-gallon of cheap red wine. The appetizer had been a tab of acid; dessert a fat marijuana joint passed around the table. Two candles stuck in empty Chianti bottles provided ambient lighting. The sound of ocean waves gently washing onto the shore came through the open windows as Miles Davis's *Sketches of Spain* played on the turntable. Joe and Barbara, who also had an apartment above the merry-go-round, were our guests. Joe worked as a hairdresser at Los Angeles's I. Magnin department store. Barbara had left her older, very rich husband to live with Joe. She was a model and wore beautiful clothes, although on this night she just had on an oversized man's shirt barely covering her thighs. I wore a T-shirt dress that barely covered mine. Our lovers sported cowboy shirts and jeans as we sat cross-legged and shoeless on the floor.

Suddenly, the front door flung open. A dark figure stood in the doorway holding a gun, growling, "Hands up." Was this a hallucination? We stared in stupefied silence as a man in a black scuba suit, complete with skin-tight cap, goggles that almost covered his face, and flippers, flapped his way into the room. He reached down and wrenched the remainder of the joint from Joe's fingers.

"Simon!" my lover exclaimed, as Frogman took a toke of the roach.

"Aw, man, how'd you guess," our next-door neighbor said, removing his goggles and pushing back his diving cap after he passed the joint back to Joe.

"The gun," Roy replied. "No one else I know has a Luger semi-automatic that his father took off a captured German sub-mariner in World War II. Want some spaghetti?"

Simon tried to sit cross-legged, but it was hard for him to bend in the rubber suit and flippers. In the end he joined us at the table wearing... nothing.

# Spring Cleaning

*Joan Osterman*

What's all this clutter?
Rusty regrets, expired goals.
Where rage burned,
smoldering coals.

Disappointments—
rake into piles.
Family secrets—
stash in files.

Outdated emotions—
time to diffuse them.
Set them out at the curb;
someone could use them.

# Stormy

*Lisa Gibson*

My Uncle Snip had been bragging about Stormy all day. As the grownups got deeper into the cocktails, the wonders that Stormy could do grew more and more implausible.

We were on holiday, and I was swimming with my brother Garth and cousin Heidi. Neil Diamond's *Hot August Night* played in a never-ending circle of vinyl until someone, usually a prune-fingered kid, turned over the record for "Cracklin' Rosie." We could easily pilfer food, and Aunt Bette always heated the pool to at least 85 degrees to keep us children in the water and out of the adults' hair.

It was windy and cold at the top of the pool slide, but from there, we could see over the fence to the field and barn where Stormy the Wonder Horse lived. A long wooden ramp joined the field with the pool patio. My brother was atop the slide when Uncle Snip went muttering down the ramp and up to the barn.

"He's gonna do it!" my brother yelled. He slipped down the slide and splashed into the warm water.

"I think he's serious." Heidi announced while climbing the ladder. Slip, splash.

From somewhere in the house, Aunt Bette cried out, "Oh god no! Snip, please don't do it, we believe you."

Climbing the ladder, I alerted the two in the water, "Here they come!" Horse and rider appeared from up the ramp. Uncle Snip was in full cowboy regalia. With glass in hand, he was sitting easy in the saddle. "You guys better get out," I hollered from atop the slide before pushing off. Slip and splash.

Stormy didn't hesitate until she hit the patio. The path of small, glossy pebbles was slick for a horse wearing iron shoes. Heidi and Garth, dripping and shivering, stood out of the way, wrapped in their towels. In the deep end, I clung to the side of the lima-bean pool and watched. Uncle Snip urged Stormy down the pool steps in the shallow end. It was clear that she did not want to get into the pool. Brown eyeballs rolling, nostrils flaring. Stormy reluctantly followed Snip's urging. He was humping the saddle, leaning back, gently squeezing with his legs and giving her just a hint of heel as he was talking to her; her ears, facing backwards, listened as his soft voice spoke only to her.

"Come on. Good girl. You can do this. Let's show these sons of bitches why you're the best goddamned horse that ever was." Deliberate and delicate as a ballerina *en pointe,* Stormy chose her way down the steps.

Most of the grownups were standing silently, mouths agape, cocktails forgotten. Other uncles, each wearing a championship buckle—now a sliver of silver glimmer under bellies made round and soft from age and liquor—toasted that relationship between a damn good rider and a truly great horse.

When Stormy had all four hooves on the bottom of the pool, she paused. The water reached Snip's boots and her belly. She settled, looked across the pool seeming to assess the situation— then she simply walked until she was swimming in the deep end.

"We got it now, girl," said Snip. Stormy circled the tiny deep end and again found footing in the shallow end. She was a different horse getting out of the pool; though her load was made heavier with water, she didn't mince or struggle. All hesitation disappeared as she muscled her way up, showing the power and manner of a true Grand Champion.

"I told ya she could do it, ya fuckers!" The horse spooked a bit at my uncle's loud whoop. The grownups remained frozen in place. Garth and Heidi ignored the film of saddle soap and horsehair that now coated the pool water and leapt in. Stormy slipped a bit on the patio, got her footing, and tried to break into a trot. Keeping her in check, Snip calmly rode her down the ramp.

The grownups went inside as I climbed the ladder, and despite the chill, I had to pause. Looking out over the field and up to the barn, I watched my uncle unsaddle Stormy. He wiped her down, then brushed her. When he bent to inspect a hoof, I could tell by the way she leaned her weight on him that he was forgiven. The glow of the sunset through the cocktail glass resting on the fencepost caught my eye. I watched the sun setting on a cowboy—with his face pressed against the face of the best goddamned horse that ever was.

# Third Flight: Challenges

# I Hear America Weeping*

*Peggy Prescott*

I hear America weeping, the varied cries I hear,
Those of children cowering in classroom, waiting,
The parents sobbing as they measure the coffins,
The concert crowd turned to terror as bullets rain down,
The Rabbi reeling as he folds notes for the sermon unspoken,
The frightened worker diving for safety as shots ring outside,
The young black man, still half-citizen, always fearful, vigilant,
The woman, tortured in a man's body, fighting to be known,
The abandoned elder, choosing between meal or medicine,
The kids warned not to play outside, not to drink the water,
Each crying for what should be theirs
as nights brings new darkness and when the cries quiet,
we search again to find the words, to find the song.


* *An update for Walt Whitman*

# A Lesson Learned

*Sarita Lopez*

Ms. Beril Burnaugh had been teaching sixth grade at Connecticut's Center for the Blind for less than two months, but she was already beloved by students and faculty alike. Her fellow teachers knew three things about her: She was smart, witty, and well-dressed. Her students also knew three things about her: She was patient, smelled like vanilla mixed with orange-scented marker, and had a voice that could make even the most ADHD-child settle down. Three things no one knew about her: She could speak eight languages, had at least fifteen aliases, and was one of the most sought-after assassins-for-hire on the dark web.

Beril had landed difficult jobs before, but this one was a doozy. Even more difficult than when she had put a bullet between the hazel eyes of Paulina Sokolov—her only friend in the world, and also her lover. Paulina had had the unfortunate luck of stumbling upon Beril's unlocked safe, which contained multiple passports and currency from around the world. Or the year before that, when Beril had been paid a delightfully obscene amount of money to take out Rwanda's Prime Minster. She'd had to take a job as a cleaning woman in his house just to be close enough to drop a few milligrams of a highly concentrated nerve gas in his morning oatmeal. He was found hours later, slumped over a toilet, bloody vomit pooled around a once-white fuzzy bathmat. No, this job made others in the past look like child's play.

The teaching certificate was an easy forgery. Learning enough Braille to get by took discipline, but thanks to YouTube and Google, it hadn't been impossible. Killing old Mrs. Nelson, the original sixth-grade teacher, had been a breeze—just a smear of liquid cyanide on every piece of mail Beril grabbed out of the educator's rusty mailbox ensured that the octogenarian's thin skin would quickly absorb the poison. Mrs. Nelson was so old that no paramedic or coroner would question a sudden, and fatal, heart attack. All of the signs pointed to a quick job with a fat paycheck. So, why was this particular contract so hard to close?

Five months ago, Beril (then known to her Swedish neighbors as Helga Adell) had awakened to a soft "ping" coming from her laptop. This meant just one thing: a new target. Her eyes widened as she entered in her passcode and read the message. "No shit," she had whispered as she took in the details. The hit was on one of her own—a skilled assassin who was known in their circle as the Black Widow. If one was good at one's job, there would only be rumors about said colleagues; but real names, living arrangements, known family members, or—more importantly—what said assassin looked like, were never revealed. Those rules were thrown out the window when a target was placed. Beril took in a photo showing a man and his daughter, smiling for the camera. The Black Widow's name was apparently Jasper Declan, age thirty-seven. Good looking, with salt-and-pepper hair; tall enough to lie and pass for six feet tall (the profile had him at just under), and a chin dimple that reminded Beril of an L.L.Bean model she had masturbated to as a tween.

The message listed all of the useful information. Along with a street address and floor plans, Jasper appeared to be a single, gay father to a twelve-year-old blind girl named Scarlett. Apparently, he had made today's list because he had been sloppy and pissed off the wrong person. Beril had made mistakes in her many years on the job, but Jasper must have made too many obvious ones to be on such a blast.

"PAYOUT IS $250,000.00 USD. MUST COMPLETE MISSION NO LATER THAN SIX MONTHS FROM TODAY. MUST BE A PAINFUL DEATH. OTHER FAMILY TO REMAIN UNHARMED. DO YOU ACCEPT?"

Beril had felt the rush of giddiness that came with every new job. She had gleefully clicked "ACCEPT," before shimmying her way to the fridge to open a new bottle of Russian vodka, which she bought once a month to remind herself of Paulina. She poured herself a stiff four fingers' worth as she planned on how to enter into Jasper's life. She already had ideas on how to end him.

For being stupid enough to be caught, only the most agonizing poison should be used. She would use something so new it didn't even have a scientific name yet, just a very expensive price tag. The Saudis called it "Kiss of Death," and Beril had been waiting for the perfect person to use it on. She almost salivated, thinking of how she would film Jasper as his blood vessels burst inside him, one by one. He would cry tears of red as his body convulsed, before most likely biting off his tongue in the final acts of a seizure. It was a shame she couldn't do the same to his daughter, but rules were rules, and she had messed up too many little times to add another mistake to her roster. A six-month lead was longer than usual, and she had been confident she could do it even sooner.

With less than one month left on the contract, Beril was tired of wearing Laura Ashley and having to make small talk with Jerry Menegon, the math teacher who spat when he spoke and seemed to be unaware that nose clippers existed. The easiest part of the whole charade, surprisingly, was being Scarlett's teacher. The girl was quiet and shy and didn't need attention, unlike some of the other youngsters in the class. The hardest part was getting to Scarlett's dad.

So far, Jasper Declan had been impossible to poison. She'd caught glimpses of him when he would pick Scarlett up from school—and once tried to shake his hand in introduction (with a small swab of her special poison taped to the inside of her middle finger)—but he had kept his hands in his pockets, saying he had a cold. She had rubbed the Kiss of Death on a permission slip and carefully slid it into a clean envelope, so that Scarlett would be unaffected, but the slip came back signed, no blood splatters in sight. She tried scheduling a parent-teacher conference, and a nanny appeared instead. Beril had gritted her teeth while sitting through that one, never wanting to kill somebody so badly.

Now, five months, nine days, and sixteen hours after first receiving instructions, Beril felt desperate. The message said that the death needed to be painful—but as long as Jasper was dead, would the powers-that-be really care how it happened? Making up her mind, she decided to get this hell over with that night. Pillow over the face, or a "robbery gone wrong"? She would have to choose at random, even knowing that such impulsiveness would unleash inner turmoil.

In the cover of darkness, she parked her sensible Prius five blocks away from the Declan residence. It was past one in the morning and Beril checked to make sure there were no lights on, not even the blue glow of late-night television. With the coast clear, she quickly picked the simple lock and slid inside. She took off her shoes, wiggling her bare toes to be as quiet and nimble as possible. Beril then began to creep upstairs, where she knew, from months of studying the house's layout, she would find Jasper's bedroom.

"Hello?" a soft voice appeared to her left, just as Beril was about to pass by a doorway. Scarlett's bedroom. "Is... is someone there?"

Beril held her breath as a skinny white cane shot out from the door. It brushed Beril's foot as it swept past. A few more taps and Scarlett seemed to be satisfied that she was alone. The cane went back inside—and Beril allowed herself a small breath, as she snuck past until she was at Jasper's room.

*Should I use the knife? Or the pillow? Oooooh, or strangle him with some minty floss?*

She could feel herself sweat as the excitement grew. Her palms were slippery and her tongue dry as she stepped inside. She wiped her forehead and blinked away the heavy perspiration.

There was no bed. In fact, the whole room was empty. No Jasper. No furniture. Not even a pillow to use for smothering.

"Expecting something else?" A voice from behind made her already fast heartbeat double. She turned.

Scarlett stood in the doorway, smirking.

"What the—?" Beril took a step forward and stumbled. Her vision became blurry, her legs weak like half-cooked noodles. "Did you... did you do something to me?"

Scarlett held up the seeing-eye cane, a tool it was now obvious she didn't need. "Hope you don't mind, but I borrowed a bit from that little jar you've been carrying around. You should really be more careful with your things." She continued to smile.

Beril's mind flashed to when the cane had grazed her bare foot. "Kiss of Death..." She began to cough wetly. "You little BITCH."

"Not so little actually. I just look *very* young for my age. I would give you a warning for next time, but I think we both know there won't be any more jobs after this. You've become messy in your work. The bosses aren't happy. They gave you one more test—take out Black Widow. You were even given a photo. But you didn't stop to think there were *two* people in the picture—me, and a man the bosses hired to pose as my father. A little sad to know I'm growing up in such a sexist world." Scarlett sighed. "Oh well, having that quarter-million dollars will be nice at least."

Beril tried to take a step forward, but her eyes were already murky with broken capillaries, and the pain of her insides melting was excruciating. She collapsed on the ground, convulsing in agony.

Three things flashed in her leaking brain before taking her last breath: She really hadn't minded wearing pastel cardigans; Braille had been more complicated to learn than any other language; and last, but not least—she would finally be with Paulina.

# One Night

*Edgar Calvelo*

Midnight wind
like a hundred galloping horses
tears through the woods

breaking trees, felling power lines
like moments of sudden insight
sparks sprout

bloom

trees light up
hiding the stars
blaze dances, laughs, gathers energy

hellish hilarity,
fire pours its peaking power
descends
the valley sleeps below

immobile, innocent, whole neighborhood
stands alone in its path

leave, hurry, unprepared, dazed

helpless

swift in devastation
ashes, uninterrupted silence

morning comes

fields of desolation

grief, too heavy
even for God
to carry.

# I Have the Hair of an Old Woman

*Judy M. Baker*

I have the hair of an old woman.
It doesn't seem to fit my face.
Diminished, tinged with gray,
heir apparent to burnished coffee-colored tresses,
falling like a faint echo as faded as the vibrancy of youth.

Brown spots dot the back of my hands,
soft reminders of my years on Earth,
nestled among freckles populating hands, arms, legs, and face.
Supple, sinuous shoulders, sturdy legs, bendy torso,
a strong core,
betrayed by feet and hands afflicted by confused,
muffled tactile signals,
balance demands full attention—being present in a way never
   imagined when it came with ease.

Bald for a year, grateful for the return of hair upon my head,
teased by a permanent envy of women with lush, long locks.
These days, my curls come in a box,
ordered online, delivered by post.
Whimsy inspires changing my look to suit my mood,
while I long for healthy tresses flowing from my scalp,
   cascading down my back

Re-sprouted hair arrives, soft white fuzz,
giving way to a shock of silvery gray,
supplanted by lively coal-black curls, soft as silk.
Metamorphosis upon metamorphosis,
curl and color appear, melt away,

ultimately revealing straight, deep-brunette strands,
sprinkled with gray.

One eyebrow grew back, the other refused to match,
a lopsided pair, compatriots of my stunted eyelashes.
Cosmetics stand in for natural fullness,
a minor inconvenience

Thinking my follicular challenges permanent,
a passing comment catches my attention.
With dreams of hirsute restitution,
I embark upon a morning ritual—coffee laced with collagen.
A few months pass before a subtle transformation,
new hair sprouts at my hairline,
and my pesky eyebrow fills in a bit as well.
Imperceptible to most people, for me, it feels like a miracle.
Proud of the gray streaks flowing from my temples,
a familial signature connecting me to my parents and sisters.

I have the hair of an old woman
So what?

# Hardscrabble

## *Marilyn Campbell*

E zra folds his handkerchief in a triangle and places it over his nose and mouth. He pulls it tight and ties it behind his head. He's trying to keep the dust out, which leaves him gasping for air and barking a dry, hacking cough at night. Carefully opening the door of the log cabin, Ezra peers out. The wind catches the door and rushes past him into the room, bringing a swirl of silt, and broken bits of leaves and twigs. Grandma and Maggie cry out together, their voices a good octave apart.

"Come help me, you two," Ezra yells. "Push while I pull." He steps outside and leans back into the maelstrom, using all his strength to pull the door after him. When he's certain the door latch catches, Ezra lowers his head against the force and pulls his collar up high. His eyes smart from the grit and begin watering, and his ears hurt as the dirt scrapes against them, sanding their rounded edges until they are red and rough. He no longer owns a hat. His hats have blown away.

At night when chores are done, and before prayers, Ezra remembers his grandpa's stories about the family's journey from Ohio across the vast frontier to reach this perfect spot in Oklahoma. Over the years, he had heard the same story hundreds of times, while following in Grandpa's footsteps.

"Farming is a hardscrabble life," he used to say.

"Yes, sir," Ezra would reply, while dropping corn seeds into furrows made by the ancient wooden plow. They made an odd procession: Shadow, the dun-colored workhorse, followed by Grandpa in faded blue overalls and work boots without shoestrings—and bringing up the rear, Ezra, barefooted and bare-headed.

"You were only four years old when we set foot down here," Grandpa told him. "Little Maggie wasn't even born yet."

Now, Ezra is fourteen and Maggie, almost ten. He smiles to himself when he thinks of how, even after Grandpa died, he could recite his stories word for word. He's glad Grandpa didn't live to see his crops fail with the wind blowing everything away, leaving only dust and disappointment. He would have been heartbroken. Folks have started calling Oklahoma the Dust Bowl—and, just like Poppa and Momma who left the rest of the family behind a month ago, some were moving on, heading west.

The next morning, Ezra grabs a bucket and heads for the well at the side of the house. He pumps the handle in quick, stiff jerks until the water begins to flow, then fills the bucket to the brim. He looks up briefly to survey the land, barely visible through a cloud of flying debris. A stand of poplar trees bends from the constant north-blowing wind. They are subservient, bowing to the elements like a row of servants in a rich man's house. He doesn't try to focus on the fields beyond, which once were filled with waving green cornstalks and soybeans. He doesn't need to look to know what he will find—total desolation from the constant wind and lack of rain. The land lies fallow.

Before returning to the cabin, Ezra feeds the chickens, milks the cow, and tends to Shadow. He fears the livestock may not make it through the winter, for their main source of feed—wild oats—is becoming harder to find around the homestead. Ezra can't keep taking them farther from home to graze, and leave Grandma and Maggie alone. Also, he fears getting caught up in one of those funnel clouds, the way he did last time he went to fetch the animals. When was that? Last week? A month ago? The speed of the twister dancing straight at him across the prairie couldn't have been more frightening. He had crouched down, trying to make himself compact—like a small tight fist—concentrating his weight in one spot. He hoped it would make his body more difficult to budge. But when the cyclone reached him, the roar was deafening—and the force of the wind moved him across the prairie like runaway tumbleweed. He could have been slammed against a rock or tree, and ended up with broken bones or worse—but Ezra was lucky. All he sustained were scratches and bruises.

Ezra shakes off the frightening image, and picks up the milk pail and water bucket. He tries stretching a scrap of canvas across the milk to protect it from flying debris, but it blows off, exposing the creamy liquid. Ezra gives up and kicks at the door for Maggie to open. Again, there is the struggle with closing the door once he is inside. *Always the struggle.* Grandma dips her fingers in the water as soon as Ezra puts the bucket down. He firmly removes her hands and shouts loudly so she can hear him.

"Don't drink the water yet, Grandma. Gotta let the sand settle first." He turns to Maggie. "You stay by the bucket and watch. Give Grandma a dipperful as soon as you see the specks settle to the bottom. Just like I showed you, now." Maggie nods her head vigorously. She seems happy to assume the extra responsibility.

In order to take on extra chores, both Maggie and Ezra had stopped attending school long ago. They would be needed at home while their folks are gone. Ezra was disappointed because he likes the smell of the books and the chalkboard and the flowery scent of his teacher when she leans over his desk to give him extra help. "We'll find you a new school when we get settled in a nicer place," Momma promised when they left to find work in California. Ezra asked Poppa why the family couldn't all go together.

"Grandma's too old to take a road trip, Ezra," Poppa said quietly one night so no one else could hear. "Her joints creak awful when she walks as it is. Can't have her falling or breaking anything."

It was true, Ezra thought at the time. Whenever she sat down, she was like a bundle of sticks falling in on themselves.

"It will just be for a little while," Poppa promised, "and we trust you to watch over her and your sister. You're the man of the house now."

Ezra felt puffed up and proud that his father was leaving him in charge.

"As soon as we find work and a place to stay, we'll send for you." Poppa said, pulling Ezra toward him in a loose hug. "Joe Reilly gave me his word he'd bring you all with his family when he heads out."

Mr. Reilly lives in town and has a much bigger automobile than Poppa's. Ezra expects he will want to leave the dry wind and ruin of the place like Poppa did. It seems like everyone in town is moving on. The phrase *Dust Bowl* pops into his head.

It wasn't until later that Ezra wondered, *"How will it be easier for Grandma to travel in Joe Reilly's car?"* Unless Poppa expects her to die, like Grandpa did.

By nightfall, as usual, they are held captive inside the dank, smoky room. Ezra notices another big crack where the wind has weakened the mud-like mortar between the logs. The sand has collected in a pile just below the breach on the plain wooden floor. He grabs a rag, wets it, and stuffs it in the crack as best he can. In the morning he will gather Shadow's warm manure and smooth it into the crack from the outside of the cabin. It will reinforce his patch job and last for a while. At least he *hopes* it will last longer than the mud he made to patch a crack once before, its consistency too sandy to hold together.

Between bouts of coughing, Ezra watches the dying embers of the fire from his cot. He remembers when he was just a little kid. *Then* he thought of the wind as a playmate. It swirled gently around him, coaxing him into an easy game of tag. Another time, when Ezra launched a homemade kite, he watched it buck and prance in the sky for hours while the stiff breeze tugged at the line. He was finally thrilled to see the wind take it to a spot so high, so far away, that he could no longer see it.

The fun stopped two years ago when things began to change. After teasing the land for a time, the wind beat down on it unmercifully. Just when he thought it couldn't dislodge any more loose dirt from the hard, cracked earth, new gusts managed to steal another inch of topsoil from the played-out fields. The land looked defeated, like an old, addled dog chasing his tail until he collapses in confusion.

After a troubled sleep, Ezra wakes to the rumbling engine of Mr. Reilly's automobile. Ezra jumps out of bed, slips on overalls, and struggles into his boots. When Ezra opens the door, Mr. Reilly is pulling his abundant weight from behind the driver's seat and struggling to keep his wide-brimmed hat on his head. He meets Ezra's gaze briefly before announcing, "Got a note from your Ma."

Ezra nods and feels the excitement surge through him.

"They sending for us then?"

"Well, not exactly." Mr. Reilly takes his hat off and clutches it close to his chest.

"They ain't ailing, are they?" Ezra asks, allowing a new fear to surface.

"No. Don't think so. Hard to tell in a note though."

Ezra kicks at the dirt with the toe of his boot, the way he'd seen Poppa do.

"Your Ma and Pa have had some bad breaks. Pickers wages aren't as good as they thought—leastways not at the place they're at. Car broke down so they can't move on just yet." Mr. Reilly mops his forehead with a rag-worn handkerchief before going on. "Your Ma said you all better stay put until they find a better spot."

Ezra breathes a sigh of relief. At least they're okay. *It will just be a little bit longer before they send for us.*

"The thing is," Mr. Reilly begins, "We got to move out soon, so if your folks aren't ready for you, we can't wait."

Were his folks abandoning them? Were the Reillys? Ezra turns away.

"But I'm sure you can hitch a ride with another family when the time comes, Mr. Reilly says. "I'll have someone come out and check on you soon."

Ezra's eyes begin to tear. He rubs a fist across them before turning back.

"Okay. Thanks," he yells, as Mr. Reilly lumbers back to his automobile.

Ezra frets about what to tell Grandma and Maggie. He throws his head back to search for a hopeful sign—something that promises an end to this hardscrabble life—but all he sees is another cloud of dust heading their way.

He turns the door handle to go inside when he hears the car door slam, followed by the sound of the engine.

# Crossing

*Kathleen Chance*

I do not want to leave.
The girl saw her people in the village below,
dancing to soundless music
in thanks for her short life.
She could see smoke and red flames of a fire
but could not feel its warmth
or smell the flesh of the roasting goat.
She reached and called.
No one answered.
Not even Older Brother who,
in white shirt and dark pants,
went to a school made of bricks.
He could read and shared books
with her on a woven mat by lamplight.
They were in the middle of a story
of a girl who gleaned wheat
and slept on a threshing floor.
Now she would not know the ending.
Mist gathered to make a cloud.
She saw gentle drops fall
on her people in the distance.
Rain would bring good crops
of potatoes and soybeans,
lessen the work
of weeding sorghum and groundnuts.
Rain would be a blessing for Older Brother,
head of the household since the passing of Father.
Now she would go where he could not.
To Father

or another Father, she did not know.
Rain was falling.
A goat had given birth.
She had heard the newborn's feeble cry.
Solace on the way to her ancestors,
dancing in steam on the mountain.

# Okmulgee

*Jennifer Sullivan*

It may be difficult for younger generations to believe, but during the Great Depression of the 1930s, I happily spent the first five years of my life in Okmulgee, Oklahoma. The town was so small and rural that the only doctor had been hired by the Santa Fe Railroad to patch up guys in the section gangs, who were laying rails and repairing tracks outside of town. That railroad doctor was summoned to our house after my mother had been in labor for three days; with forceps he yanked out my brother, leaving both mother and baby the worse for wear. Little wonder that my mother was distraught when she discovered I was on the way. My birth a year later was somewhat easier, however, as she was given large doses of ether during her labor. The trauma came later—all of her hair fell out—and when it regrew, she no longer had wavy blonde hair. It was straight and brown.

My father was the assistant superintendent of the Phillips 66 Refinery, and we lived in a company compound of five houses: square boxes covered with gray wooden siding, but surrounded by gay flower beds of zinnias and nasturtiums and trumpet vines. A wide gravel drive lined by poplar trees ran below the houses; immediately beyond, fenced and gated, loomed the refinery, mysterious with white plumes of vapor rising from the cracking towers, a red-orange gas flame continuously burning high into the sky, and an odor of rotten eggs drifting out of its interior as oil was digested into gasoline.

Because we had no television, video games, or cell phones and were rather isolated in the compound, my brother Jerry and I had to invent much of our own entertainment. A particularly memorable occasion unfolded one morning at breakfast. Mama was smiling and gay in a pink housedress with green rick-rack binding. "You children have been so good and grown up lately, I have a surprise for you." She opened a paper bag and withdrew two pairs of blunt-nosed scissors, the kind we'd been using at Miss Dillingham's kindergarten. We'd wanted scissors for a long time, but Mama said we weren't old enough to use them properly. Now she handed each of us a shiny piece of magic.

We beamed. "Thank you, Mama."

"I'm happy Miss Dillingham taught you how to use them." She kissed us on top of the head and gave us some old newspapers to cut. We sat on the living room floor slicing the paper into long, ragged strips to flutter when we ran, and fashioning big, lopsided circles with eyeholes for masks.

After a while, Jerry gazed at me. "Jinny, can I cut your hair?"

I finished a diagonal slice through a large sheet of newspaper. "I don't think Mama would like it."

"She won't know. I'll just cut a little piece." He moved closer.

I thought it over. "You can cut mine if I can cut yours."

Jerry nodded, "Sure," and snipped. A chunk of blonde hair fell onto the shiny hardwood floor.

I felt my hair. "Does it show?"

"Naw."

"My turn." I raised my scissors, cut off a red curl.

Jerry touched his head. "Is it okay?"

I nodded.

"I'm cutting another piece." More blonde hair dropped.

"Now me." Another red curl amputated.

Fascinated by the slight grinding sound of the scissors through hair, and by the certain knowledge that what we were doing was wrong, we cut a great deal of each other's hair. Time passed.

"Children! What *are* you doing?" Mama stood in the living room doorway. "You've been cutting your hair!"

We glanced at each other, at helter-skelter patches of scalp and missing hair, at red and blonde mounds littering the floor.

Mama was getting angry. "I see I can't trust you after all. I thought you were more grown up." She took our scissors, stood thinking, then turned away. "Come with me."

We followed Mama out of the room, out of the house, down the brick sidewalk. The elm trees soughed, the birds stopped singing, the puffy white clouds edged away. At a wide step, Mama stopped and picked up a brick from a derelict pile nearby. Anxious, we silently watched. Mama put one pair of scissors on top of the step and brought the brick down. With a sharp breaking sound, the scissors fell into pieces. She pounded again; the shiny blades and handles disappeared. She put the second pair of scissors on the step, and once more came the horrible breaking sound. Tears ran down our cheeks as we watched, petrified....

At last Mama dropped the brick, red-faced and out of breath. "Maybe by the time your hair grows out you'll know what to do with scissors. We'll have to see." She shook her head.

"Now march. I'm going to wash your hair and see what I can do with it." She strode away, her pink housedress with the green rick-rack now a banner of danger.

Tears still on our cheeks, we looked at the rubble on the step, which was all that remained of our precious scissors. We slowly followed Mama up the sidewalk, into the house, and past a scatter of red and blonde hair.

A questionable entertainment of a different kind lurked below the gravel drive at the back of the compound: Greasy Creek, a stream of sludge released by the refinery with an oily sheen and steep black banks. To frighten ourselves, we'd stand close to the edge and contemplate the horror of falling in. Greasy Creek flowed out of the compound and ran beneath a railroad trestle, over which freight trains ran periodically. Through the fence behind the garage we could see the trestle with tracks leading we weren't sure where. One afternoon, after daring each other to walk across the trestle, Jerry and I squeezed through a hole in the fence. We climbed up a grade to the tracks, stepped out onto the elevated trestle, then slowly inched from one tie to the next. Below, Greasy Creek rolled deep and dark and evil-smelling. If we misstepped, we could slip between the ties and fall in. Or, trapped on the trestle, we could be run over by a freight train. Vaguely aware of these dangers, we were thrilled by our bravery. As we reached the other side, we continued to walk along the tracks and saw a hobo camp spread out below. Men were lying under trees, sitting around little fires with tin cans on top, smoking, talking, sleeping. We stood staring, watching these men who didn't seem to have anything to do or anyplace to go—hobos as they were called then, who sometimes came to our back door, whiskered and shabby, asking for something to eat, and Mama would give them a plate of food. When a few of the men called to us, we turned and trotted away—either too shy or frightened to respond—toward a road that led back home.

Not all of our days were filled with that kind of excitement but, rather, moments of joy to cherish. In the summertime I would wake to see sunlight streaming through the trumpet vine and hear Helen singing "Jesus on the Main Line" as I smelled bacon frying. Like the sun rising every morning, Helen was a constant in our lives. Tall and beautiful, with black skin and brown eyes, she cooked and cleaned and took care of us. Our mother didn't know how to cook, so she made menus and bought groceries; Helen did the rest. When she went home early on Sundays, we had to do with bread and milk for supper. Once in a while, Helen would let Jerry and me go home with her when she had a few hours off in the afternoon. She lived in the "colored" part of town in a small house with her mother, Sylvia, who was tiny and stooped and gave us cold sweet potatoes to eat.

Another fond memory that stands in contrast to the fancy pools of today was of a summer when the fathers had an oil tank cut down and brought into the compound for a swimming pool. They placed it between the drive and Greasy Creek, dumped a truckload of sand in the bottom so it would seem like a lake, and filled it with water four or five feet deep, over some of our heads. Jerry and

I knew how to dog-paddle, so we were allowed to go to the pool once we had on our wool bathing suits and were coated with olive oil, Mama's concept of sunscreen. One day we hauled a wash boiler over from beneath the clotheslines to use for a boat. It was a tight fit, but after squeezing in, you could use your hands to paddle around the pool. We took turns, sailing back and forth, until someone's dad arrived. "You kids could drown if that thing capsized," he shouted, and confiscated our craft. Until that loss, we had a great time.

In contrast to our current fancy parks, a frequent gathering place lay beyond the last house of the compound in a large grassy area that was used for picnics and parties. On the Fourth of July, tables were set up and everyone in the compound came, plus friends and relatives, bringing food, along with fireworks to shoot off after dark. Jerry and I would start the Fourth by lighting a firecracker under our father's bed while he was still asleep. Whether he actually was or not, he always reacted satisfactorily, whooping while throwing the covers into the air. Then, all day long, we children exploded long strings of green-and-red lady fingers that would rat-ta-tat-tat-tat in a series of explosions; or firecrackers, wrapped in purple or red or green tissue with dragons on the front of the package, that blew tin cans into the air and small chunks off the sidewalk.

The picnic started late in the afternoon with treats we rarely saw: fried chicken, deviled eggs, potato salad, Jell-o salad, sliced tomatoes, watermelon, chocolate cake, tubs of homemade ice cream. As night descended, the men lighted giant pinwheels they had attached to the fence, and fountains of silver and gold whirled out into the darkness. Parents lit Roman candles and sparklers and gave them to the children. Mama persuaded me to hold a Roman candle but, unfortunately, instead of shooting balls of colored fire into the air, it backfired onto me. For a short while, I was part of the fireworks.

One of my favorite times of the year was when the circus came to Okmulgee, arriving in railroad cars that unloaded outside of town, a magical event at the time that no longer occurs. On circus day my father came home early. "Let's go, kids. Time to watch the wagons unload." Off we'd go to see lions and tigers, monkeys and baboons roll out of the freight cars and over to the circus grounds. Elephants, led to the big top area, would heave enormous timbers into vertical position, pulling the canvas of the big top up into a huge tent, and then set up tents for the menagerie, for the sideshows and, off to one side, tents for the performers. Older kids earned free tickets, carrying water for the elephants and hay for the horses. Everywhere was the smell of the animals, the shouts of the roustabouts, the bright, shiny red, orange, purple, and blue colors of the wagons. The next day Daddy would come home before noon, calling "Who wants to see the parade?" We'd hustle downtown and line the sidewalk with other onlookers. "Here they come," we'd shout, as beautiful girls on horseback, clowns with red noses, elephants decked out in tapestry robes, tattooed men, dwarfs, and a sword swallower from the sideshow passed by. Later, at the circus performance, we cheered when the trapeze artists whirled around their ropes in great arcs, swung through the air from the arms of one to another without a net. We laughed at the clowns crowding into a tiny car, spilling out the other side, falling over their flapping shoes, chasing each other in circles; we clapped as the ringmaster snapped his whip at the lions and tigers posed on perches around him; we marveled at the horses leaping through burning hoops, standing on their hind legs to the trainer's commands. When, at the end of the long afternoon, the three-ring circus was finally over, we wobbled out of the big top full of popcorn, sticky with cotton candy, and sound asleep before we got home.

It was early one fall, when I was almost six, that we moved away. Slowly, regretfully, inescapably, those golden, carefree days in Okmulgee were overlaid by a different kind of life—days of school, of homework, of chores, the hard, rough-edged days of growing up. But I shall always cherish the thrills and joys of those early years in that tiny town.

# Monsters

## *Diego Roberto Hernandez*

All is Black except for the two groups.
Perhaps it's just as well.
I see only what I need to see.
To one side, there are the Monsters.
The Vampires, the Werewolves, the Demons.
Ghosts, Goblins, Ghouls. All that has ever hid
in woods, jungles, and caves.
Every being to have ever lurked inside closets,
underneath beds, beside sharp corners.
The Nightmares of Humanity. All those that have gone bump
in the Night or belong to the Night.
I look at the other group. They are the Humans.
They are those I have ever known, and they are those
I will never know.
They are those to whom I speak every day.
They are doctors.
Murderers.
Teachers.
Rapists.
They are the ones who give everything
they have to those who need it most.
They are the ones who step on as many
Flowers as they can.
So many claim to be angels.
Too many turn out to be Devils.
So many claim to want heaven.
Too many choose to rot in Hell.
I turn and walk with the Monsters.
At least They know who They are.

# Fourth Flight:
# Transcendence

# New-New World Symphony*

## *Marianne Lyon*

Do you think
there is anything
not attached
by an unbreakable cord
to everything else?

When I hold this query
I hear something like music
rise steadily inside
a melodic theme
that might erupt
into wild crescendo
or maybe a slow legato
burning-spill

This dusk
I walk on companion path
inside my favorite
time of day, thinking of
cities I have lived—
Hong Kong   Brussels
countries visited—
Zimbabwe   Congo

Remember these places
swallowed in
setting sun brilliance
how fiery-evening-miracle
ignites for everyone
so faithfully magical

I ask
what if we are all
but single notes
trembling offstage—
muted thunder
waiting to be acknowledged
harmonized   fashioned
into one hallowed symphony?


\* Inspired by Dvořák's Symphony No. 9, *From The New World*
*(New World Symphony)*

# The Virtues Project

*Peggy Prescott*

---

*Trailing clouds of glory do we come*

— Wordsworth

*What if* the spirit beings were watching
Earth in dismay, and agreed on 52 virtues
that were sorely needed here

*What if* they gathered together, recruited
52 volunteers willing to descend to Earth,
always a difficult tour of duty

*What if* each volunteer was given a role,
randomly assigned a place, a personality
as if preparing for a parlor game

*What if* they knew these details meant nothing,
for all that really mattered was the word whispered to them
just before they slid down from the heavens

*What if* that word was their real task,
an assigned virtue, the seed of healing they must grow
'til their outer ego withered in irrelevance

*What if* they gave themselves nine Earth-months
to prepare for their roles and all the pain,
pushing as they emerged was only a preview

*What if* that first bellow of outrage signaled
the beginning of forgetting, and all the rest
was only the struggle to remember

# How Artemis Discovered Her Immortality

*Amber Lee Starfire*

Do you believe in fate? I was a new intern at the magazine, fresh out of school, anxious to impress, and so I just happened to be the one who answered the phone that day. I'll never forget it.

When the caller told me who she was and what she wanted, I almost hung up on her. What a mistake that would have been! No one would have blamed me if I had, though. I mean, who's going to believe some random person who claims to be a four-thousand-year-old Greek goddess? Yet, there was something about her voice that stopped me. It was birdsong and morning light and wind chimes, all at once. Chills ran up my arms and prickled the back of my neck, and I just knew—deep down *knew*—that she was the real deal.

She said it was time to set the record right. That we'd been wrong about her—wrong about all the gods. She offered the magazine an exclusive, said she wanted the world to know the truth, and then she asked me a question that changed my life.

*Would you like to write my story?*

So there I was, a week later, fidgeting nervously with my pencil as I sat across from Artemis in the interview room. She was still gorgeous after so many years. Tall—at least 5'10"—her blonde hair fell in full curls on the soft, cream-colored linen draped over her shoulders. When she first walked through the door, I was surprised that she didn't look much older than I was. Except for her eyes. Looking into those eyes was like diving into deep water or falling through time. A fierce power radiated from her as she began to speak.

She told me she was born in a small fishing village, south of what would later become Athens, around 2000 B.C. I asked her about the events surrounding her discovery of immortality, her move into the nearby hills, and her subsequent career as goddess of the hunt and protector of women and children.

My own brothers were jealous of me, and it was they who began the rumors that I was unnatural and a witch. Then the village had a string of bad luck. The fish disappeared from the ocean; the deer and rabbit from the forest. Even the dadonut, a small nut that was a staple of our diet, was becoming difficult to find.

One day when I was twenty-five, the villagers, in a fierce rage led by our shaman, swept down on our house during the predawn hour. They dragged me from my bed and brought me out, naked, into the cold. They bound my father and brothers, threatening to kill them if they tried to protect me. Father pleaded for my life, not stopping until they cut off his tongue and flung it into the sea.

I closed my mouth, which I suddenly realized had been gaping open. I managed, "That's awful! What happened next?"

Rank with the kind of fear that creates such mobs, they bound me to a tree. They beat me with sticks and threw stones. The pain was horrible. The strange thing was that, even though I was bleeding copiously, I did not become weak or faint as one would expect.

I had long hidden the fact that I healed at an amazing rate. When I was a child, if I cut myself, I would bleed a little and then the cut would close. Within a minute, my skin would be completely healed. I had sometimes scraped myself on rocks or fallen and bruised myself. Always, within minutes, my wounds would be gone. I was in my mid-teens before I understood that not everyone healed like this.

When I was tied to that tree and savagely beaten, I did not yet know the full extent of my powers, but I realized the villagers would not stop until I was dead. A strange, disembodied calm came over me like a warm blanket, separating me from the fear, and I knew what needed to be done: I feigned death.

"How did you accomplish that?"

Pretending to be dead is not as easy as it sounds. You can't just close your eyes and go limp. They'll only think you've fainted and wait until you wake up to keep beating you. I rolled my eyes up into my head and, with the strength of my will, slowed my heart until its beating was as faint as the whisper of a dandelion. I made my breath so shallow that even the shaman was unable to detect it. They finally stopped, but they set two men to watch over my body, so "the witch won't get up and walk away."

She laughed then—a golden, warm laugh that made me want to lay my head on her lap.

As if they could keep me! The rope that tied me to the tree had loosened during the beating. I waited until my watchers fell asleep and slipped out of my bonds. I snuck the hunting knife from the belt of one of the men and the spear from the ground by the other while they snored like the idiots they were.

I looked one last time at my home, its occupants sleeping in the darkness; at the beach, where I had spent most of my childhood—and I fled into the woods, where I learned to fend for myself and to hunt.

The rest, as they say, is history.

Artemis smiled gently at me, her ocean-blue eyes glowing with a hint of sadness.

The gods, you see, all began like me—human, with homes and parents and siblings. There is just one small difference between us and the rest of you: we cannot die. Life just goes on and on and on.

That was the first of my interviews with Artemis, which led to my career as storyteller for the gods. But that first conversation is burned into my memory. You see, I had never thought before about what it would really be like to discover you were immortal, and separated forever from the rest of humanity by lifetimes of time.

Have you?

# Collect My Dust

*Dana Rodney*

God
When I die
Collect my dust
But do not remake me a woman
Make of me a stone
A rock reposing on the lap of the earth
Unnoticed
Elemental
Resplendent in the frigid moonlight
Empty of utterance
Of no particular use
Except perhaps to toss into the sea
One ecstatic splash
The only word I speak

# Begin with Plants

*Bonnie Durrance*

To learn to love, begin with plants. Spare animals and other humans the insult of your expectations. Love needs acceptance. Better to start with plants.

Plants are easy to accept. Here, for example, on the northern California coast, there is a humble little plant called a coyote bush. It is a small-leafed, scrubby survivor-of-a-thing that hunkers low on sea-facing hillsides, and consorts with mobs of blackberry brambles—forming dense, impenetrable, tick-riddled thickets. I never thought much about the bush until now. Now, it's October; a hot, spare, month. Nothing seems able to breathe, much less bloom. Then one day, before my very eyes, the sun moves in behind a coyote bush, firing up the little furry flowers and setting the bush into a visual blaze. In that moment, everything changes, and I realize I can love this bush: not for its fruits, for it has none; not for its rampant, high-colored blossoms, for it has none; not for its shade, nor for its graceful branches, nor for its mythological connotations, for it has none of these; but because I have seen it in its true glory.

Plants teach us how to live and let live. They let us fail at commitment without felonious consequences. You leave a faithful schefflera in a house on another coast, and it suffers—some renter may sear it in too much sun or drown it in too much water—its collapse is not something you will build your life around preventing. The plant is free to live or die. You may surround yourself with cheery things in pots and then forget all about them when you go into a decline. No matter. Plants are used to the moods of nature. While they might wither in protest or give up entirely, you will not be arrested. Plants are willing, like certain qualities in the soul, to come back and try again, when we are ready.

And if they don't, we can forget them—as we never can forget the person who did not return.

Plants teach tolerance. Think of the tiniest ones, the white ones that come up like stars on the floors of the Eastern spring woods, or the gentle violets that poke through cracks in our neighborhood's sidewalks. We would not insult their innocent faces by calling their colors inadequate. Or suggesting they didn't make us happy. Or saying, "You should see the flowers in California!" Never. There is no confusion: Plants are not you. You do not mistake your inadequacies for theirs. You never think to berate them for not pleasing you more. They are only what they are. And you don't lay your life's hopes on them and feel that through your love, your perseverance, your insistence the coyote bush, say, will become a rose.

Loving plants is natural. So much easier than loving people, with all their faults. You, for example. You, breathing heavily in the night close to my ear so I cannot hear the wolf howl from across the mesa. You, with your sneezes that buckle the walls and scare the birds out of the bushes in the garden. You, who never listen.

I am thinking of your flaws as I tend my dormant phalaenopsis. I study its brilliant pink blossoms with their monkey faces and lascivious tongues. I remember your smile, as you fill the living room doorway holding out a bouquet of roses. I remember you saying, "You look nice." I remember you there on the couch, quiet for once, bending over your drawing, with your notebooks strewn around your feet, looking the way you probably looked at six. And I smile.

Maybe I should try to love you like a plant. Then our love would be easy. Tend and care. Live and let live. Enjoy. Even with one such as you, who, if you were a plant, would be a jungle.

# Patina People

*Antonia Allegra*

Once a million years ago
    Last week
I felt close to all people
    to speak, to whisper dreams,
    to hum magical tunes
    to wonder.

Now, since going through the door, a change
A new understanding: the universal range
    of loving all people
    is still there…
    I still care
But it's the patina people
    who really speak to me.

Those people worn around the edges from loving,
Their brilliant shine dulled by years of giving
Their immediate smile speaks of sincerity.

They are the real people,
    their numbers are few,
    but their loving influence
    is the strength of many.

The patina people are the past,
    for without it, they would not be
    so strongly in the present,
    shining for us all.

And the future… yes, they are there,
For patina people never leave us.

# The Living Truth Detector

*Geoffrey K. Leigh*

Almost five adventurous years have passed since Pablo was born to Emilio and Sara, an intended conception with unexpected consequences. It was a normal birth, and all systems in little Pablo's body seemed to be functioning well as far as medical professionals were concerned. But apparently, there are some systems for which the scientific community does not perform tests. Nor do they realize their existence. Emilio and Sara, however, experienced the results of just such a mysterious and perfectly functioning system.

Sara and Emilio met in college while Sara was studying medicine and Emilio was exploring painting and sculpting. They fell madly in love and were married after Sara's residency at UCSF. As both were from the Bay Area, they decided to stay near family. They eventually settled in Napa, allowing Sara to join a cardiology practice and Emilio to teach part-time at the college while also continuing his creative endeavors.

When Pablo was conceived, both were happy at the prospect of starting their family. They wanted to continue their careers while also spending as much time as possible with their new baby. Sara stayed home for two months after Pablo's birth, then Emilio took the lead caring for their son when Sara was working. After the first year, they arranged to have an au pair from Panama come to cover hours so his parents could have more focused time on their careers and have consistent care for Pablo—and Pablo could learn to speak more Spanish.

For the first three years, Pablo seemed on a path of typical development. He was a happy baby, and as he got older, he started spending time in Emilio's studio. Emilio created a work space shortly after Pablo's first birthday by separating off the third-car portion of the garage. He installed a room air conditioner, an additional north window to improve the light for painting, and a separate entrance. Now that Pablo was four, he and Isabel, the au pair, explored Emilio's trove of art supplies and materials.

"Ah, Emilio, maybe you want to come see this bowl Pablo made," said Isabel with some hesitancy in her voice.

Emilio put down his brush and walked over to the wheel where Pablo and Isabel were working. "Did you make that, Isabel?" Emilio inquired.

"I turn the wheel, but Pablo made the bowl!"

Emilio heard the words, but he had a hard time believing them. "Really? You didn't help him?"

"No, Pablo made the bowl."

Emilio continued to stare at the nearly perfect bowl that Pablo had created. "Wow, Pablo, that's terrific! I'm amazed at how quickly you've learned to make pottery!"

"Because I used to make this stuff when my family lived by the water. But we had to kick the wheel."

Emilio and Isabel both looked stunned. Neither knew what to say as they continued to stare at the bowl.

"Well… I guess you kind of remembered," stammered Emilio. He looked imploringly at Isabel, but she didn't know what to say either. "Nice work, Pablo." Not quite knowing what else to do, Emilio went back to his painting, but his mind was somewhere else the rest of the afternoon.

When Sara got home, Emilio told her about the experience he had with Pablo and the bowl.

"He said what?" quizzed Sara.

"He said he used to make these things when his family lived by the water."

"Oh, he is just sharing one of his imaginary stories. I think you are overreacting, Emilio. You can't take a four-year-old that literally. Their brains are developing and they are still learning," explained Sara, relieved that it was nothing serious.

"You think so? You think he's just being creative? He sounded so definitive when he said it," continued Emilio.

"Come on, honey. There's no other way to explain it."

"Ok; you know more about this than me. But still, there was conviction in his voice that sounded unusual to me. It was really odd and surprising."

"But that is how kids relate to fantasy. They can sound very sure of themselves, even when it isn't true," replied Sara, wanting to put the issue to rest.

Emilio let the discussion die at that point, and yet it didn't feel finished to him. He began to read about children who reported past-life experiences, and how some of the information they shared was verifiable and accurate.

Several days later, Emilio decided to ask Pablo a few more questions regarding his other life. "I've been wondering about your life by the water. Can you tell me anything else about the place that you remember?" he asked in a matter-of-fact tone, or at least with as much casualness as he could muster under the circumstances.

"I remember a few things. I had some brothers and shared a room with two of them. My father went fishing, and we ate lots of fish and fresh fruits. We wore looser clothing. And there was a castle thing at the edge of the water where it was fun to explore and play games." Pablo responded again in a matter-of-fact manner and exhibited the same confidence.

"Do you remember the name of the town where you lived?" inquired Emilio, increasingly curious about this whole affair.

"No, not really. It was like Saiba or Saida, something like that," Pablo replied. Then he went back to a drawing he was making.

The next morning as Sara and Emilio were having coffee on the patio, Emilio shared his interactions with Pablo. "I think he really does remember some of these things, much like in this book I have been reading about children reporting past-life experiences. I think it would be interesting to investigate this further," said Emilio with some excitement, as if he had discovered a new painting technique he wanted to pursue.

"Let's not get too excited about this," chuckled Sara. "Pablo has a terrific imagination, which is wonderful. I don't want to squash it. But I also don't want to reinforce such tales and encourage them any further. It will only make it more difficult for him to make friends and relate to teachers."

"Ok, but I still think there is something to this," responded Emilio, as a final parry just before losing the fencing match.

Emilio and Sara said nothing more about the incident, nor did they ask Pablo anything further about his reported memory. Still, Emilio kept reading about children who made such reports and wondered about the possibility of Pablo's story being accurate. He kept looking at old castles in Europe that might be near water, but none came close to what Pablo had described. Eventually, he got caught up in a new piece of art he wanted to finish, and that refocused his attention and energy.

Nearly six months later, on a chilly Saturday morning, Sara and Pablo were eating breakfast at the kitchen island. Sara was enjoying a slow morning and wanted to get several things done around the house, but she was in no hurry to get started. Her coffee was still hot, and she held the cup with both hands to warm them a bit.

"Could we go play in the park today, Mommy?" inquired Pablo.

"No, Pablo, I don't have any time to do that today. Maybe another day soon."

"That doesn't feel like the truth," responded Pablo.

"What do you mean by that?" asked Sara indignantly.

"I see this cloud come over your chest, and I feel it in *my* chest. It feels like you're hiding something. I remember that cloud like I remember living by the water," answered Pablo.

"Well, I'm not. You're simply mistaken," replied Sara rather sternly.

"Ok," said Pablo as he slid off his stool and headed for the garage door and the studio.

Sara was stunned by this sudden encounter with her young son. She reflected on the many things she wanted to get done that day. She had told the truth. *And what right did Pablo have to question his mother*, she thought? She continued to sip her coffee and felt the correctness of her statement. Yet something was nagging at her, something unsettling.

It only took three more sips of coffee to turn on the lights: she *did* have time to go to the park, but she also had other plans and things she would rather do. *So we are both right*, thought Sara. But that unsettled feeling crept in again. *No, he's right. I wasn't really truthful. I wanted to do something else, but I didn't want to explain myself. I didn't want to have to justify doing what I wanted to do rather than go play in the park.*

While the story of living by the water was surprising, knowing when someone was not telling the truth was even more unnerving and shocking. She had no idea *anyone* could do that!

Sara finished her coffee and turned to her tasks for the day, feeling the urgency to get the things done. As the day went on, she felt more settled regarding the way things had gone with Pablo. *Besides*, she thought, *he probably doesn't really know, or will remember, what went on between us this morning. He's just a child, after all.*

A few days later, Emilio and Pablo were in the studio, Emilio working on his canvas and Pablo continuing to sketch with black ink and paper like Emilio had shown him. After some time, Emilio moved to stretch and take a break. He wandered over to see how Pablo was doing and was surprised. There, on the paper, was a drawing of an old castle surrounded by a body of water. Emilio stared at the drawing. He was sure he had seen something like that before, but he couldn't remember where. It looked a bit Roman, maybe with a Middle Eastern twist, though he wasn't sure why.

"Very nice, young man. Where did you see that picture?" asked Emilio.

"I saw it when I lived near the water. It's like the building we had in our village."

"Son, that's very well done!" Emilio still recognized a similarity with some image he had seen, but he was unable to connect it with an artist. He walked over to his computer, then sat down and scoured the Internet for some clues. Emilio started looking through pictures of castles in the UK, France, Spain, and other parts of the Mediterranean. Finally, he came across a well-known Scottish artist, David Roberts, who made many drawings of places and people in the Middle East. As Emilio was going through Roberts's work, he stopped suddenly and stared at a picture entitled "Citadel of Sidon." There, from a different angle and more elaborately rendered, was a castle very similar to what Pablo had drawn. Emilio looked further and found another Roberts drawing of Sidon. This one had a view similar to Pablo's drawing but at a greater distance from the Citadel. Still, the similarity was amazing.

Emilio asked Pablo to come look at his computer. Pablo put down his pen and walked over, then looked at the drawing by Roberts. "Nice, Dad. That artist must have lived in the same town as me." Pablo headed back towards the table where he was working.

"Wait, Pablo—come back for a minute, please." Pablo walked back over and looked up at his dad. "Have you ever seen this picture before?" inquired Emilio.

Pablo looked intently at the computer screen, then turned back to his dad. "No, Dad. But it's very nice," replied his son.

Emilio went back to the first drawing he had found and asked the same question.

"Nope, not that one either. But I like this one more. It's a better drawing of the building."

"Ok, thanks, son. You can go back to your work now." Emilio didn't know what to think. Had his son seen the drawing somewhere? Was he just copying what he saw? But how would he remember so much detail? Emilio was familiar with Roberts's work from art school, but he was sure he didn't have any copies of this work around the studio or house.

Emilio walked back over to Pablo's work table to look at the drawing again. "How's it coming along? You about finished?" he asked.

"Almost. I'll finish today."

"May I take it when you're finished? I would love to put it in a frame, and hang it in the hallway next to the painting of the old Paris street I did last year. Would that be all right with you?"

"Sure, Daddy. I'd like that."

Later, Emilio want back to his computer and printed out the two drawings by Roberts. Then, after Pablo finished his piece, he took them, along with Pablo's work, to show Sara.

"This is the drawing of the castle in the village by the sea that Pablo mentioned last year where he learned to throw pots. He finished it today. Then I showed him these two drawings by David Roberts. They're of the Citadel of Sidon, which, in Arabic, is pronounced Sayda. Roberts made them in the 1800s."

Sara studied Pablo's drawing, then looked closely at both prints by Roberts. "Do you think he saw these prints somewhere before?"

"I asked him that, and he said no. I don't see how he could have, either. I know about them from my classes, but I don't think I have any copies of them here," responded Emilio. He looked a bit shocked still.

"I don't know what to think," remarked Sara hesitantly.

As Pablo came in from the studio, Sara looked at him, half smiling. "Great drawing, honey! Now I believe what you said about having lived by the water before."

"That doesn't feel true, Mommy."

Sara took her last sip of tea while reflecting on what she just said. "You're right, Pablo. I *want* to believe what you said about living by the water before, and it's difficult to believe that children remember such things as past lives. But I promise to work on it, because I love you and I'm clear that you tell the truth. But knowing that someone can tell when someone else is telling the truth may be an even bigger challenge for me."

Emilio leaned over and gave Sara a sideways hug. "It isn't easy for me either," he said to Pablo. "And I appreciate the evidence you gave us to help with this shift in learning what children can do." Then Emilio turned to Sara and looked into her eyes. "Do you remember a primary request you made when we got married? What you asked for in this relationship was 'All the truth, all the time.' I guess we got a reminder of how to incorporate that more pervasively in our lives!" chuckled Emilio.

Pablo walked over to them. *"That* feels like the truth, Mommy and Daddy," he said with a smile.

# Tapestry

*Jim McDonald*

You peer at poem
just rendered on page,
mere early draft,
a little rhyme, not too much
the look, hours, touch
a bit of metaphor or simile
skate on ice, sliding
along life's edge.

Words morph in context
couplets into longer stanzas
one direction leads to another
dust off surface debris for
hidden meaning lost over time
archeologist of memory.
Is the poet in control
or does poem write itself?

Scribble thoughts in darkness
comfort of bed left behind
capture those dream fragments
inner thoughts otherwise lost
slide toward soft slumber
awaken to daylight ready
to weave threads into cloth,
tapestry of verse.

# Grandmother of God

## *H. Martin Malin*

It is searingly hot today, as if Satan has unstopped the chimneys of Gehenna. The desert air is filthier and fouler than the inside of a buzzard's mouth. The caves give some respite from the dust and the wrath of the sun but do not provide much comfort.

When I pray these days, I am more downcast than ever. *Elahi* has surely turned his back on his chosen people. The pestilent Romans He has visited upon us are as thick as flies on rotting mutton.

They harry us for their own sport. When they discover one of our caves, we are forced to gather our meager belongings and flee to another. No matter. We know these labyrinths far better than they.

Our men are scattered to the far reaches of the desert. We women are old now. Most of us are widows and no longer much endangered by the Romans' insatiable lust for blood and sex. In the past, when they would catch us, they would force us to pollute ourselves with each other for their amusement, on pain of death.

But such depravity only bores them now. They long for the inexhaustible pleasures of Rome: the circuses, the gladiators in the arena and the public baths, the nubile slaves and temple prostitutes with whom they can debauch themselves.

We old women now bear helpless witness to an age of abject misery and despair. Rebellions against the Romans smolder and periodically burst into flame, only to be viciously snuffed out. Tales concerning my grandson Yehoshua fuel the zeal of foolhardy rebels and grow ever more fantastic in the retelling.

And thus, I have determined to set down a record of what I have seen with my own eyes and heard with my own ears, a testament of truth which perhaps will die with me in these caves but, if it be the will of *Elahi*, may be read by others in more fortunate times.

I am called Hannah, by some called Anne, daughter of Issachar and Nasaphat of the lineage of David, wife of Joachim and mother of Maryam of Nazareth and grandmother of Yehoshua ben Yôsēp, murdered by the Romans.

When I served *Elahi* as a virgin in the Temple I learned many things from the priests and scholars, among them how to scrape and cure animal skins to make parchment for their scrolls, and how to make ink with the soot from the smoke of oil lamps. These skills now serve me as I write on parchment I have prepared from goat skin, with ink I have made from the substance of smoke and the colors of the earth.

I learned from the priests how to seal writings in clay jars and hide them in the niches of caves so they will not be destroyed by vermin or the elements and will be safe from the Roman occupiers.

For did not Moses the Patriarch show his aide Joshua, Son of Nun, how to take writings and anoint them with oil of cedar and seal them in an earthenware jar? Did Moses not teach Joshua, who defeated the Canaanites in Jericho, how to protect the books of the law that would later be entrusted to him?

Did not *Elahi*, the Lord of Heaven's Armies, the God of Israel, instruct the prophet Jeremiah to take documents recording the purchase of fields from his cousin Hanamel and seal them in an earthenware jar so they would last for a long time? This, I learned as a virgin at the Temple.

Regard these writings that I, Hannah, leave for you sons and daughters of a more fortunate time. They bear witness to my truth.

The zealots and gossips have spread many lies. They have said that I was a virgin when I conceived Maryam of Nazareth, as she was a virgin when she conceived Yehoshua.

They have said that Maryam remained a virgin after the birth of Yehoshua ben Yôsēp, as attested by the midwives Zelomi and Salome, and when Salome inserted her finger into Maryam's parts after Yehoshua's birth to ascertain her virginity, her hand was burned and withered as punishment for her lack of belief. None of this is true.

The gossip these jackdaws spread that Maryam did not suffer throughout her labor and remained a virgin following the birth of the child are falsehoods. I, Anne, was her only midwife. There was spilling of blood and pain during the delivery of Yehoshua my grandson, as there is with the birth of every child.

Nor, when we rested in a cave on our escape from Herod's bloodthirstiness, fleeing from Bethlehem to Egypt, did Yehoshua leave his mother's breast and walk on his own legs to confront fearsome dragons and command them not to harm us. Neither did lions and panthers walk with us on our journey, wagging their tails as harmless pups, larking about among the oxen and the asses.

All of these falsehoods and more have the zealots and gossips told about my grandson.

They have said that while he was a babe in Egypt, he entered the temple at Sotinen, in Hermopolis, and three hundred fifty-five idols prostrated themselves before him and broke themselves into pieces. And that Affrodosius, governor of the city, arriving at the Temple with his entire army intending vengeance, fell on his face before Maryam, with my grandson in her arms, and worshipped him as the one true God.

These fools have said that when Yehoshua was a four-year-old child in Galilee, playing at the River Jordan with some village children, he made seven pools of clay with passages for water into which he brought a torrent from the river, filling and draining the pools as he commanded. They have said that one of the children destroyed his pools and Yehoshua cursed him as a son of Satan, killing the child with his voice.

They have said that the boy's parents, with a gathering of Jews, raised an outcry with Maryam and Yôsēp, and that my daughter admonished Yehoshua not to do such things lest he make trouble for himself and his family. They said Yehoshua then kicked the dead boy in the buttocks and raised him from the dead.

They have said that Yehoshua then took clay from the pools and made a dozen sparrows. When Yôsēp reproved him for unlawfully doing work on the Sabbath, they said my grandson clapped his hands together and the birds came to life and flew away.

They have said that the son of Annas, the High Priest, came to destroy the pools that Yehoshua made and that my grandson cursed him and suffered him to wither and die on the spot. When the child's parents demanded that my family leave the village, Yôsēp warned my grandson that he was turning the townsfolk against him, so Yehoshua lifted the dead boy by the ear and spoke into it, whereupon his spirit came back to him and he revived.

None of these things are true. Absolutely none of them.

What is true is that Yehoshua was a difficult child, disrespectful of his teachers. He was sent away from their schools again and again. He refused to do his lessons and made no secret that he knew more about every subject than his teachers. Yehoshua often told his parents that he was not their son.

Maryam spoke to him. Yôsēp spoke to him. I spoke to him. None of us could convince Yehoshua to cease provoking others with his insolence, especially his enemies among the powerful in the Temple and the court of the Romans.

I repeatedly beseeched him to take care in his words and behavior for the sake of his own safety and that of our family. His response was that he was about his Father's business and that we were not his family.

Yehoshua insisted he was a mortal human and then he insisted he was not. He insisted his father was not Yôsēp ben Heli but *Elahi* Almighty. He insisted he was God himself made manifest on earth.

"Does that make my daughter Maryam the Mother of God?" I asked him sharply. "Does that then make me the Grandmother of God?"

He smiled and kissed my forehead. He gave me his blessing. He admonished me to be at peace and not trouble myself for him.

He broke my heart.

And so, I sit in this cave and write what I know to be true and what I know to be false.

We Jews are no threat to the empire of Rome, but they are determined to grind us to dust. They have long since corrupted our priests and rendered the Temple a holding pen for the sheep our venal priests have become. The Romans despise us Jews and count it their pleasant duty to make us as miserable as they can without exerting themselves too much.

Many sabbaths have now passed since my grandson, Yehoshua ben Yôsep, was hideously tortured and slaughtered on a cross at Calvary, a punishment Rome reserves for terrorists and criminals who are not citizens of the empire. My daughter Maryam looked on in horror. She has never recovered. She is utterly broken.

She would not have me stand beside her as her son was murdered—so I watched, and wept hysterically, from the shadows. Praise be to *Elahi*, the God of Abraham and Isaac—if there be such a God—that Yehoshua ben Yôsep died after suffering for only six hours. The rabble was disappointed that he died so quickly. The Romans know how to make the ordeal last much longer; sometimes they prolong it for days.

My grandson was condemned as a seditionist by that outcropping of Roman excrement Pontius Pilatus, betrayed by our own High Priest Yôsep Caiaphas and his night soil in the Sanhedrin, our rabbinical tribunal.

If I had been able to advise my grandson before his trial, I would have begged him to keep his counsel, as I have done so often before. But he would have ignored me. He was as headstrong as a goat. It was the arrogance of the Roman blood in him.

Oh yes. Roman blood without doubt. The Romans rape our virgins with impunity. It is their legal right to fornicate with Jews or any other non-citizen of The Empire without consequence of any sort. Even our young men are not immune to their perverse iniquity.

My Maryam was surely no exception, although she denies it. Yôsēp ben Heli was an old man when the Priests betrothed her to him as they forced her out of the Temple on her 12th birthday, before she could pollute it with her monthly courses. And without the protection of the Temple, she soon became pregnant—she says by the breath of *Elahi*. Maryam swears no man, including Yôsēp ben Heli, has ever come into her.

When Yôsēp found out Maryam was with child, he planned to dismiss her quietly and nullify the betrothal, as often happens in these matters. But the corrupt priests couldn't resist an opportunity to meddle once again. They summoned Maryam and Yôsēp to the Temple.

Abiathar the Priest accused my daughter of carnal impurity. Maryam swore that an Angel sent by *Elahi* told her that the child was God's own son, the long-awaited Messiah. Yôsēp swore an Angel came to him separately and told him the same thing.

Abiathar the Priest forced both Maryam and Yôsēp to swallow the Water of Drinking of the Lord and walk around the high altar seven times. But no sin appeared in their faces, and he begged forgiveness from *Elahi* for his wicked suspicions.

Women of my age have heard many stories like this. In a sheep wallow like Nazareth, a twelve-year old virgin like Maryam, sheltered in the Temple since I weaned her in her third year, stands little chance of not being defiled before marriage, whether by her betrothed, a randy shepherd boy, or an execrable Roman.

Nevertheless, we love our daughters and do everything in our power to protect them. Honor killings are a way of life among some of our people. That is why her father, Yôsēp ben Heli, sent Maryam into hiding with her cousin Elizabeth and protected her along the road to Bethlehem.

But I fear all my care for her, her children, and my grandchildren has come to little. Yehoshua cried out from the cross, *Elahi, Elahi, lema sabachthani?* Those are the words of my forebear, David the Psalmist, and they are my words also: "My God, My God, why hast Thou forsaken me?"

They are the words of my heart, as I write on these skins, anoint them with oil of cedar, seal them in a jar and hide them in this cave to keep them from the filthy Romans.

*Elahi, Elahi,* why has Thou forsaken Thy people Israel? Why has Thou forsaken my grandson Yehoshua ben Yôsēp; my grandson Yehoshua who believed he was Your son?

Why hast Thou forsaken his mother who now sits mute beside me, mired in grief? Why hast Thou forsaken my daughter Maryam, called by the zealots the Mother of God?

And why hast Thou forsaken Thy servant Hannah, who the zealots and gossips now call the Grandmother of God?

*Selah.*

# Cherub Blossoms

*Joan Osterman*

On a cold winter
tree, tiny round birds
bloom on bare branches.

Their songs flutter
skyward. My heart stows
away on their wings.

# The Dream Dies

*Sue Kesler*

I've never been into all that woo-woo shit. My opinion? You can take your ghost and shove it. At least that's what I thought until 5:52 p.m. yesterday, a day I've been reliving in my head ever since.

That was the time when I walked across a nondescript room and headed through the apartment to the dingy-walled, old-fashioned bathroom described in my guidebook. On this unplanned addition to an April pilgrimage to Memphis's Graceland while on a search for the Beale Street blues section of town, we stumbled on the Human Rights Museum, a far cry from the commercialized rock-and-roll site we'd just left.

"Yuck. Why would anyone want to live here?" I asked, but got no answer from the guy who'd crossed the courtyard with me. He'd bagged this part of the tour and left me to go it alone.

I shrugged and kept moving. Something about the room seemed wrong. The closer I got, the more my uneasiness and odd sense of reluctance grew. A small room with olive-green walls surrounded the ground-in grime of a grungy tub. Worn pink-and-gray linoleum on the floor, and battered wood around the streaked window glass, made the space more repellent—less of a space where I belonged.

"What a dump," I said aloud. I crouched down and peered through the narrow slit of an open window above the dirty wood of the sill. Seconds later, the temperature of the air around me seemed to drop to below freezing. I shivered, experiencing an intense sensation like an ice-water dousing. I couldn't move. Goosebumps sprang up on my arm and the intense chill caused me to gasp involuntarily.

In the next moment, I gazed through the eyes of a dead man as he prepared to take the life of a man across the way. I was me and not me, assuming a stance behind the filthy window over-looking the ratty 1950s motel across the parking lot opposite me. A sign plastered across one wall identified the place as the Lorraine.

"Time you fuckin' porch monkeys learned a lesson," I/he muttered, peering down our invisible rifle and lining up the crosshairs ꞌat the man standing on the balcony. My hands took the positions needed to steady the gun for the shot.

At that moment, as I readied to pull the trigger of what my logical mind told me was a non-existent weapon, the killer moved in. I felt the weight of the weapon. His thoughts became my thoughts; his hatred, my hatred; his loathing of the man who was to be his target, mine as well. The malign emanations of the cold killer with the pockmarked face I saw reflected in a faint image on the glass pane infiltrated every pore of my body. I became that killer. I was living in his world.

"That nigra bastard's gonna get what's coming to him. Actin' like he was as good as a white man. Shoulda stayed where he was. Not gotten uppity, stayed in his place. You got about two minutes left to live, boy—you interferin' son of a bitch." His words formed on my lips, my voice silent, the words unvoiced.

"Stop, stop," I screamed at the intruder in my head. "None of that is me. I'd never say anything like that. I'm only here trying to understand."

I felt his muscles tense, my own mimicking his, ready for the shot. "Take it slow, Ray—you gotta wait until those other ashy-faced cocksuckers get outta the way."

I tried to pull back, move the barrel of the gun away from the small group near the man on the balcony, smiling and waving at the crowd below. He bent forward by the railing to respond to a shout from a well-wisher. The stock stayed firm against my shoulder; the scope remained rock steady. I screamed silently.

One eye sighted the target; my finger tightened and pulled to execute the unthinkable. Time slowed as my eyes tracked the bullet leaving the muzzle to travel straight as a die to the balcony.

And the dream died.

The killer's phantasm faded, leaving me alone, my thoughts filled with the horror of the deed and my profound sense of shame that I shared the same shade of skin as the killer. I stood up, cheeks wet, and backed away from the window. I'd seen, been part of, one of the great tragedies of our nation, aware that the spirits of those who die a violent death linger.

# The Man in the Striped Pajamas

*Bonnie Durrance*

A man in striped pajamas dreams
he finds a knife in a devil's food cake.
He licks it clean and hides it in his bed.

But it's not really a bed. That's only the dream.
It's more of a mat, but that's not the point.
And the point of the cake isn't food.

Now the devil is loose in the room. He pulls
open drawers. He smokes up the place.
The man wakes and takes stock of his life.

He says to himself: if I were not in this jail
I'd know what to do with that knife. I'd cut
my shackles free. I'd take my slice of the pie.

I'd chip through this wall. Escape to the sea.
He starts to feel full and warm and he smiles.
Then he goes back to sleep and he dreams.

He sees the devil at a desk with his hat on.
A large book is open and he's studying columns.
The man stands before him. Asks what to do.

The devil looks up. He is shockingly handsome.
Your prison defines you, he says. Your plans
are like matches. They flare up and fizzle. This

scares the man stark awake. Now the room is dark.
A pinpoint of sunlight sears through a crack.
Its radiant edge ignites all it touches. The man

caught in the light, finds himself crying. Light
burns through his shirt to his heart. The walls
fall away. He listens and no longer dreams.

# The Island

*Geoffrey K. Leigh*

Water descends into the pool
tree leaves wave faintly
flowers unfurl their fragrance
birds chirp and peck
ocean kisses the beach
while a breeze embraces
us all.

My body relaxes
my feet hug the earth
blood leisurely flows
heart paces the earth beat
peace everywhere
when we foster
relaxation.

With life's assiduous business
focused on achievement
much to do
to say, to acquire
I forget to remember
the quiet possibilities of
the heart.

# Contributors

**Antonia Allegra** is dedicated to the art of the word. She is a poet, and a career/writing coach. Her years as a journalist span food, wine, and travel writing. She is the author of "*Napa Valley: The Ultimate Winery Guide.*" She also has launched three local magazines: *Napa Valley Tables*, *Appellation*, and *VINE Napa Valley*.

**Stephen Bakalyar** has had a diverse writing career as a chemist, producing marketing materials and publishing research papers in scientific journals. Now retired, he writes poetry, memoirs, essays, and short stories. He enjoys reading at the salons and open mics of Napa Valley Writers.

**Judy M. Baker,** a lover of good food and literature, reads books like many people eat popcorn. Collaboration, curiosity, and compassion describe her philosophy. Baker is a speaker, author, and book-marketing mentor. She helps authors reach more readers and builds author brands. Websites: bookmarketingmentor.com; brandvines.com; judymbaker.com

**Lynne Berghorn** is retired from the fashion industry in Dallas. She also worked as a flight attendant for TWA, based at JFK, and later at SFO working for United. She was married in London and worked as a volunteer raising money for cerebral palsy. When she returned to the States, she continued volunteering for many organizations while raising her son. She has written two poetry books: My Heart Sings and Dancing with God. She also writes creative fiction through allegories and short stories. Currently, she is working on a memoir.

**Lance Burris** is a writer and painter who lives in Napa. Much of his work focuses on the history and culture of Napa and Sonoma Counties, in which his family has deep roots.

**Edgar Calvelo** is a retired physician. He has taken classes in creative writing at Jackson Community College in Michigan and Napa Valley Community College. He enjoys playing chess. He tries to walk to the river every day, carrying a book, stopping to sit at empty benches along the way and read. He lives in Napa with his wife.

**Marilyn Campbell** draws on experience as a former social worker when she writes. She published *Trains to Concordia*, a coming-of-age story based on riders of the historical orphan train movement. The novel is used in the curriculum of a Fairfield school. Its sequel, *A Train to Nowhere*, follows the characters in their migration to California. Marilyn has contributed to the anthologies of both Napa Valley Writers and Redwood Writers as well as to small journals and reviews. Visit her website: camitzkepress.com.

**Kathleen Chance** is enjoying the writing life after a career in elementary education with the Napa Valley Unified School District. She finds it rewarding to evaluate submissions for the NVWC annual high school writing contest, and appreciates all of the literary opportunities available in Napa and the Bay Area.

**Bonnie Durrance** is a professional writer, photographer, and producer from Washington, DC; New York; and the coast of Maine. Her essays and poems are published in various journals. Her little book of limericks, *Light Verse for Dark Days*, by Spike the Chicken, can be found on Amazon.com.

**Jan Flynn**'s story "Dummy" appears in *First Press*. Other fiction appears in literary journals: *Midnight Circus, The Binnacle,* and *Noyo River Review;* and anthologies: *Into the Woods* and *Chrysalis* (forthcoming). She has won both First Place and Honorable Mentions in *Writer's Digest* national competitions. She lives in St. Helena with her husband Michael.

**Lisa Gibson** bucked her family tradition of life in the circus. Instead, she graduated from UC Davis and spent twenty years as a public school teacher. "The moment I was introduced to public education, I felt right at home. One must see the comedic as well as the macabre in everyday life." She hopes to die alone among her cats and the glitter.

**Stephanie Hawks** is a retired Music teacher from Napa Valley Unified School District. She is currently working on a memoir about growing up on the Trinity River.

**Diego Roberto Hernandez** has been published in several magazines, newsletters, and websites. He is an aspiring author who majored in English at UC Berkeley. He prides himself on being able to write about anything, but he tends to write emotionally gripping fantasy tales.

**Lenore Hirsch** is a retired educator who writes features for the Napa Valley Register, as well as poetry and stories. Her books include her dog's memoir, *My Leash on Life;* a poetry collection, *Leavings;* and *Laugh and Live, Advice for Aging Boomers.* See *lenorehirsch.com* and *laughing-oak.com.*

**Kymberlie Ingalls** is native to the San Francisco Bay Area and the creator of the successful blogs *Writer Of the Storm* and *Neuroticy = A Societal Madness.* Her work focuses on personal topics such as love, relationships, grief, and memory loss. Ms. Ingalls has a colorful history in stage, comedy, auto racing, radio broadcasting, and teaching. All of this feeds her broad scope of writing in memoir, prose, fiction, and essays. She has received praise from critics, colleagues, and readers for her heartfelt honesty and emotional depths. Ingalls currently works as a freelance editor, public speaker, and writing coach.

**Bo Kearns,** journalist and writer of fiction, lives in Sonoma, California. He is a U.C. Naturalist; a beekeeper, avid hiker, and supporter of conservation causes. For his career in international finance, he has lived in Bahrain, Indonesia, and London. He writes feature articles for the *Sonoma Index-Tribune* and *NorthBay biz* magazine. His novel, *Ashes in a Coconut,* was published in May.

**Sue Kesler,** (Estee Kessler), has had three tongue-in-cheek paranormal novels published, featuring a most unlikely detective team. The series includes *My Partner Jakup the Jay*, *J&R Rides Again*, and *Jaybird in a Lei*. Several other manuscripts are in progress including *Lakota Fall*, a morality tale set in 1962 that deals with hot-button topics facing us in the twenty-first century.

**Geoffrey K. Leigh** taught classes in human development, family relations, and marriage and family therapy at universities in the Midwest and West. He co-edited *Adolescents and Families,* and recently published a non-fiction book, *Rekindling Our Cosmic Spark.* He has served on the NVW Board, has attended the Napa Valley Writers Conference, and is working on a fiction trilogy while working locally in real estate. See *Noussentrism.com.*

**Sarita Lopez** published her first Young Adult novel, *Fauxcialite*, in 2016. Her second novel, *The Last Pageant in Texas*, will be published in October, 2019. Sarita currently serves as Vice President and Publicity Chair of Napa Valley Writers. When she is not writing, she is working on her beverage business, Green-Go Organic Cactus Water.

**Marianne Lyon** has been a music teacher for 43 years. After teaching in Hong Kong, she returned to the Napa Valley and has been published in various literary magazines and reviews including *Ravens Perch, TWJM Magazine, Earth Daughters,* and *Indiana Voice Journal.* She was nominated for the Pushcart Prize in 2017. She is a member of the California Writers Club and an adjunct professor at Touro University in California.

**H. Martin Malin** started writing fiction after retiring from Napa County as Assistant Deputy Director for Mental Health in 2014—and wishes he had started sooner. He is working on a collection of short stories about five fictional grandmothers, called *Grandmother Quintet,* and a novel.

**Jim McDonald's** poems have appeared in the 2016 and 2017 editions of the *California Writers Club Literary Review, 2017 First Press, Ravens Perch* and the *Jessamyn West Creative Writing Contest Anthology.* He writes for and is vice-chair of the town's Arts Commission in Yountville, CA.

**William Carroll Moore** is a retired architect/urban planner living in Napa. After he earned a BS in architecture at UC Berkeley and a masters degree in planning from Athens Technology College in Greece, his professional career included technical writing and teaching at Cal Poly, San Luis Obispo. He now continues writing in other genres.

**Aletheia Morden** is Vice-Chair of the McCune Foundation Board for the McCune Collection—a rare-book and arts collection located in the McCune Room of the JFK library in Vallejo (*mccunecollection.org*).

**Joan Osterman** writes and paints in Napa and Sonoma Valleys. She has read her poems at the Sonoma Festival of Light and Rhymed Verse, and the Rianda Writers Showcase. Her poetry, fiction, and memoir explore harmony and conflict. She is a member of California Writers Club. Contact her at *napa.joan.o@gmail.com.*

**Carole Malone Nelson** has published two memoirs, *Well, Now You've Done It* and *What in the World Are You Doing Here?* The former is about the twelve years on Kauai that she and her husband spent after retirement, and the latter is a traveler's memoir about their adventures to over 100 countries. This is her first attempt at poetry.

**John Petraglia** is a writer, editor, and poet living in Napa, California. He recently retired from a career in corporate communications for a global environmental engineering company.

**Peggy Prescott** retired from elementary school teaching and now works part time for Pacific Union College supervising student teachers. She has won multiple awards in the Jessamyn West Contest for fiction, non-fiction and poetry. She studied with Carl Dennis, Brenda Hillman, Jane Hirschfield and Peter Ho Davies at the Napa Valley Writers Conference and meets regularly with the Solstice Writers Group in St. Helena. Her book *Neurotic's Guide to Retirement* was published in 2010.

**Dana Rodney** is a retired Napa Valley business owner with a lifelong interest in literature and history. She currently is a member of Napa Valley Writers and Redwood Writers, as well as a writing student at Napa Valley College. She has completed a novel entitled *The Butterfly Wing*, which takes place during the founding years of the Napa Valley in the 1850s, as well as a collection of essays about growing older as a Baby Boomer entitled *Turning Into a Pumpkin*.

**Amber Lea Starfire** is an author, editor, and creative-writing coach. She has published two memoirs—*Accidental Jesus Freak: One Woman's Journey from Fundamentalism to Freedom* and *Not the Mother I Remember*—and several books on journaling. In her spare time, she also loves to dabble in fiction and poetry.

**Jennifer Sullivan** (Buchwald-Baerwald) grew up in Oklahoma and Kansas but has spent much of her adult life in California. A former UCLA faculty member, her fiction includes a novel, *The Levee*, 2013, and three short-story collections: *Afterthoughts*, 2014; *Country Living*, 2016; and *Points of the Compass*, 2018.

**Barbara Toboni** has published a variety of short stories and articles in anthologies and online including: *Cup of Comfort, Wisdom Has a Voice,* and *Sisters Born, Sisters Found.* She is also the author of three collections of poetry. Barbara's children's book, *The Bunny Poets,* was published in 2018 by MacLaren-Cochrane Publishing.

**Rose Winters** is a published and award-winning songwriter. An obsessed novelist as well, she can be found (by day) in frumpy sweaters on a laptop and (by night) out playing her original music to the awesome people of Napa Valley. Musings and music can be found on *www.rosewinters.com.*

Made in the USA
Lexington, KY
19 November 2019